THE EARL'S TIMELY WALLFLOWER

Taken by Destiny, Book 1

By Aurrora St. James

DRAGONBLADE PUBLISHING, INC.

ARE YOU SIGNED UP FOR DRAGONBLADE'S BLOG?

You'll get the latest news and information on exclusive giveaways, exclusive excerpts, coming releases, sales, free books, cover reveals and more.

Check out our complete list of authors, too!

No spam, no junk. That's a promise!

Sign Up Here

www.dragonbladepublishing.com

Dearest Reader;

Thank you for your support of a small press. At Dragonblade Publishing, we strive to bring you the highest quality Historical Romance from some of the best authors in the business. Without your support, there is no 'us', so we sincerely hope you adore these stories and find some new favorite authors along the way.

Happy Reading!

CEO, Dragonblade Publishing

CHAPTER ONE

Present Day
Kentucky

T HE BRIGHT JINGLE of the shop bell rang out as the last customers left, each with a small bag of books. Lily Bennett waved and smiled until they were out of sight and then breathed out a sigh of relief. After three years of moving around, she'd been so certain that this was the place where she could feel at home, but as the late afternoon sun shone through the windows, lighting up the floating dust moats, Lily second-guessed herself. Again.

Bookhalla was a small, dusty bookstore filled to the ceiling with books new and old. Bright gold lettering on the front window beckoned to people browsing the small shops on Main Street. Stained wainscoting lined the lower walls with a muted green paint above, and stuffed club chairs invited guests to linger, read, and breathe in the comfortable scents of old paper and leather. With Lily's love of books, it should have been her dream job. Instead, it did little more than pay the rent on the ratty apartment that her landlord thought was a mansion. It certainly hadn't settled the restlessness that continually stirred in her chest. Corbin Kentucky and Bookhalla were supposed to fill that void, not crack it open wider.

She pushed away the pang of odd emotion and sat at the mahogany monstrosity that her boss called a desk. Cranks raised the desk top up and down to different heights, tilted a section into a drafters table, or raised a bank of drawers in the back that were otherwise hidden. It had more gears than her watch. Somehow, it suited Mr. Samuel perfectly, like his own personal Frankenstein.

Lily retrieved her cell phone from the purse that she'd stashed beneath the desk. Her belly fluttered as she turned it on. Despite her misgivings about Corbin, she'd mustered her courage, and the last of the money from the sale of her parents' home and put in an offer on a three-bedroom cabin on the river. It would be a new place for her to call home. A place that *felt* like home. Hopefully, it would be one that Archer and Bellamy would come back to as well. They needed to be a family again. Her brother and sister were all she had left.

She glanced at the glossy fashion magazine on the desk as she waited for the phone to start. Her little sister, Bellamy, graced the cover in a tiny, sapphire-blue Louis Vuitton bikini, splashing through clear aqua water in a tropical paradise. With long, blond hair, blue eyes, a willowy frame, and legs for miles, photographers practically salivated to book her.

Lily pushed her glasses up on her nose. At five feet three, even though she had a decent hourglass figure and wavy, caramel-brown hair, she'd always been invisible next to her sister. Not that it mattered. Bellamy lived in New York now. The last man to pay any attention to Lily had constantly picked at the way she looked and how she dressed. He wanted a beautiful, elegant woman to hang on his arm at parties, not a nerdy wallflower who still didn't know what she wanted to be when she grew up. A woman who found more excitement in her romance novels than she ever did in real life. He wanted a woman like Bellamy.

Lily stuffed those thoughts away with all the others that kept her awake at night and tucked the magazine into her purse. She was proud of her sister for reaching her dreams. If a bit of envy tinged that pride, she ignored it. Just as she dismissed the pangs she felt whenever she thought of the silly, childish dreams she once had. Besides, it was a waste of time to mourn a past that couldn't be changed. All she could do was see to the future. One that would hopefully bring her remaining family back together and settle the ache in her chest that left her feeling *lost*.

Lily jumped when her cell phone rang in her hand. For half a moment, she hoped it was her older brother, Archer, finally returning her calls. Last year, rebels attacked his Navy Seal team, and his physical injuries ended his military career. Lily didn't know any of the details, only that after months in the hospital, he was now stateside and refusing her every effort to talk to him. It appeared that now was no exception.

"Hello, Mr. Samuel," she said, hoping her boss didn't hear the disappointment in her voice.

"Lily, I forgot the rental contract for Mr. Pederson, and he's a bit put out. Can you find it and bring it to me?"

She pressed her lips together, trying not to laugh. Ely Samuel would forget his shoes if they weren't already on his feet. He owned the building and was attempting to rent out the space next door. "Of course. Where do you think you left it?"

He paused, and in the background, she heard the clink of dishes and silverware and the dull conversation of a restaurant. "It must be in my desk. I couldn't have left it at home, could I?"

Anything was possible, she thought. "I'll find it. Where shall I bring it?"

He gave her the name of a restaurant in the nearby town of London and hung up.

She spent a couple of minutes searching the various drawers at the front of the desk before giving up and retrieving one of the metal cranks. At first, it didn't budge, but with some pushing, pulling, and a little bit of swearing, Lily turned the gears that lifted the back set of drawers into place. The first few held some paperclips, an old metal bottle cap, and a cat toy shaped like a mouse. The last drawer only opened an inch.

Lily frowned and stuck her finger into the gap, feeling for something that could jam the drawer. A plastic pen shifted, giving her another half inch. She put two fingers into the opening, feeling around the sides and top of the drawer. Her fingers brushed over cool metal on the left, and she pushed at it, though the angle was awkward and made the wood dig into her hand.

Click.

Lily paused. The metal piece had barely moved, yet she'd heard the sound distinctly. Still, the drawer wouldn't budge. She ran her fingers through the space one last time, telling herself that this was ridiculous. Mr. Samuel wouldn't go through all this effort to file a contract, would he? *Hmm. This was eccentric Mr. Samuel. He probably would.*

At last, she found the pen jammed against the top of the wood. A bit of maneuvering and it slipped down, freeing the drawer. Lily pulled it open. Inside lay the contract.

"Of course," she murmured. As she took it out, the back of the drawer caught her attention. She didn't see the metal piece she'd pressed and a chip in the wood of the back wall showed a dark space behind. On instinct, Lily pulled the drawer further out. She sucked in a surprised breath. The drawer had a false back wall that hid a compartment only four inches deep. In it lay a dusty, black velvet box.

It appeared to be a very old jewelry box of some kind. She should leave it alone and close the drawer, but curiosity trampled common sense faster than she could consider the consequences. Lily set the contract aside and picked up the box. Tingles raced over her arms as she imagined what treasure might lie within. A bauble for a lover? A medal from a war hero? She opened the lid and gasped. Nestled on a bed of black satin lay a small, red enamel egg with gold filigree. She lifted it out of the box, surprised at its weight. It was perhaps two inches tall and an inch in diameter, easily fitting into her palm. Miniature gold hinges and narrow, vertical lines of gold hinted that the little egg opened down its center.

It was the loveliest thing she'd ever seen, much like the famous Fabergé eggs in its detail. Lily slipped a fingernail between the gold sections and gently opened the egg. Mauve silk lined the inside shell and revealed a gold clock face with two little figurines beneath. No, two *dancers* of considerable detail. A man in a suit with tails reached his arms toward a slim woman. One of her hands held the skirt of her gown to one side, and the other reached for the man. Behind them was a round opening where she could see the inner workings of the clock, and it appeared as though a metal bar moved the figures. Her breath caught. Did they dance together at a certain time? Maybe on the hour?

How long had this little egg been hidden in this drawer? Did Mr. Samuel know of it? It seemed unfortunate to leave it tucked away for years, never seen or admired for its unusual beauty. Breathless, Lily sat up straighter. Maybe she could finally repay him for his kindness. He'd been the only person in town willing to give her a job. The people of Corbin were friendly, but wary of strangers. She'd almost been forced to move on, and then Mr. Samuel offered her a part-time job.

A bookstore seemed so ideal. Books had been her only escape from the grief of losing her parents a week after graduating high school. With Archer on secret military assignments, she became the sole caretaker of a teenage Bellamy at the height of her rebellious years. The only way Lily could visit exotic places was in the pages of a book, preferably romance, where conflicts were resolved and everyone lived happily ever after.

Lily tucked the egg back into the velvet box, grabbed the contract, and put both into her purse. Gathering up her keys and phone, she locked up the store and headed for the restaurant in London to drop off the contract.

Probably the closest I'll ever get to the real London.

Half an hour later, after she had delivered the contract to Mr. Samuel, Lily parked her battered old Honda in front of her apartment and shut the car off. She did a quick search but didn't see anyone lurking nearby. With luck, she'd make it to her apartment without bumping into either her creepy landlord or her ex-boyfriend. Both hovered around her door more and more frequently. Even though it was an unseasonably warm day for October, a shiver tracked down her spine. She quickly locked the car, and all but sprinted to the stairs.

Two flights up, Lily let out a sigh of relief to see her doorway empty. Then her landlord stepped out of a shadowed alcove a few feet down from her. It was clear that he'd been waiting for her. Lily's stomach flipped over, and her mouth went dry. Squaring her shoulders, she power-walked to her door and ignored the man heading her way. Her fingers shook as she found the apartment key on her key chain. She stabbed the key into the lock and turned it just as the overwhelming smell of sweat, beer, and cigarettes hit her.

"Lily," her landlord rasped. He was only a few years older than her, probably in his early thirties, but his hair was thinning, and the lines on his face made him look closer to forty.

She thrust the door open and hurried inside, calling out, "Sorry, Dennis. I have to pee!" She slammed the door in his face and engaged the locks before sagging against the wall.

"Come see me, Lily," he called. Several horrible, phlegmy coughs sounded, then he added, "We need to talk."

God, she had to buy that cabin. She couldn't stay here any longer. Besides the exorbitant rent, the apartment was smaller than the bathroom in the house she'd grown up in. She had just enough room for a foldout bed, a small table with two chairs, and a bookshelf. The only closet was the linen closet in the bathroom, which was barely wide enough for a folded towel. The kitchen could be traversed in three steps and boasted such luxuries as a half-size stove with only two burners, a microwave that couldn't fit a big coffee mug, and a refrigerator not much wider than her hips.

Lily set her purse on the table, pulled her phone out, and checked her email. Unfortunately, there was no news from the realtor. What if she'd been outbid? What if the owners didn't want to sell to someone who hadn't lived in the town for more than a couple of months? No, she just had to be patient. This cabin would be a place of comfort, not just for her, but also for Archer and Bellamy. They needed that. *She* needed that.

Her stomach chose that moment to give a very loud rumble, reminding her that she'd only had an apple for lunch. She opened the freezer, moved the broken ice tray aside, and got out a microwave dinner. While it heated, she fished under the bed until she found the small parcel of tools. During her brief stay in Tennessee, she'd tried her hand at making jewelry to sell online for extra money. She hadn't made enough to even break even on the supplies. At least the tools might finally come in handy with the little clock.

She laid a soft cloth over the wood table, then carefully opened the velvet box and removed the delicate egg. The dim dining room light didn't diminish its beauty. It needed cleaning, but Lily feared ruining it. Instead, she opened the tool bag and selected a pair of tweezers. Pushing up her glasses, she opened the egg and carefully moved the clock hands. The little dancers clicked but didn't move as the minute hand reached twelve. As she suspected, they should dance when the clock struck the hour.

She found the latch that exposed the inner workings of the clock and was surprised to find a small crystal at its center. *Hmm, maybe that's part of the decoration.* Lily studied the movement for a few moments, uncertain what she was looking for. She was about to close the clock case when she spotted the little bar under the female dancer. It should connect to the gear behind it as it had with the male dancer's, but had slipped off. With exquisite care, Lily used the tweezers to reconnect the bar and closed the case. Holding her breath, she wound the tiny spring and saw the gears begin to turn. The minute hand moved and the watch softly ticked.

Lily's fingers shook as she moved the minute hand around to just before twelve. With luck, the little dancers would come together. From the placement of their arms, it looked like they might stand close. Lily bit her lip and nudged the hour hand onto the twelve.

One second passed. Two.

Then the male dancer moved to the middle of the open space, and the female joined him. His arm raised up to take hers, and they slowly began to spin. She laughed in delight as the dancers whirled around on an invisible dance floor. White light glowed behind them, making the gold of their bodies shine. It pulsed brighter.

Lily blinked against the glow. Then light flared from inside the watch, blinding her. She tried to stand, to back away, but her feet tangled in the legs of the chair and she fell backward. Scrabbling to catch herself, she reached out blindly but found only air. Pain shot up through her backside as she hit the floor, and before she could process it, her head struck the corner of the bookcase. Her vision blurred. Then darkness took hold and dragged her under.

STEADY POUNDING ROUSED Lily back to consciousness. She blinked and shielded her eyes from the light. Thick, gray clouds covered the sun, yet it seemed unusually bright and turned her stomach. She heard several voices but couldn't make out their words. The stench of rotten garbage filled her nose and mouth, making her gag. She tried to turn away from the smell, but tilting her body that way made her fall to her hands and knees. The pounding was louder here. Taking a shaky, shallow breath, she blinked to clear her vision. Several pairs of leather shoes moved past, but none stopped.

Lily forced herself back onto her heels and looked around. Everything was fuzzy and a bit blurred. Her head throbbed, and she felt nauseated. A woman and a young girl hurried by, wearing flowered bonnets and cloaks over colorful gowns.

What the... where...?

She turned her head to look around, but the sudden movement made her want to vomit. She breathed through the pain until her brain could right itself enough to make sense of what she was looking at. Lily knelt on a sidewalk between two shops. The buildings were either brick or simple wood structures. The alley behind her was the source of the rotting stench. Men in suits with long coats and beaver hats walked beside women in long gowns. Several buggies were parked along the street, and a horse and carriage rolled by. A few people cast her alarmed glances, then rushed past. The skies chose that moment to open up, and cold, fat raindrops sank into her clothes and skin.

Lily pushed to her feet, swayed, and found her balance. It took longer to settle her stomach, and she pressed her fingers to the throbbing in her temple. Another pounding ache was making itself known at the back of her head. She lifted her other hand and winced when she found a large knot and her fingers came away red with blood. As she watched, the steady rain rinsed her fingers clean.

Nearby, a loud, clattering sound made her jump. Lily spun toward the noise, stumbled on unsteady legs, and stepped into the road. A horse whinnied. Someone shouted, and the black blur of a horse and coach heading directly for her finally registered in her sluggish brain. She threw herself back toward the sidewalk and landed in a crumpled heap. Pain shot through her arm. Her stomach heaved from the sudden movement, and she swallowed several times to hold back the bile.

Lily sucked in a deep breath. Before she could right herself, a crowd had gathered, and a pair of blurry white boots stopped beside her.

She looked up, winced, and grabbed the back of her head. Two images of a woman appeared, wavering until they merged into one person, a young woman, looking down at her with alarm.

She said something, but Lily couldn't make out the words. Her ears rang, and her head throbbed. She tried to shake her head, but that only made the nausea worse. The woman reached down and gripped her arm, helping her to stand. A man wearing some sort of blue uniform was at her side in seconds, and between the two, they loaded Lily into the black carriage.

"Wha...?" she slurred.

The coach lurched forward, jarring her abused body. Dark spots danced before her eyes until the carriage faded into a gray, blurring sea of pain.

October 1813
Hawthorne Hall
England

GABRIEL HAWTHORNE, THE fourth Earl of Rothden, placed the last shotgun back in the case with the others and closed the glass door. He'd cleaned all twelve in anticipation of the house party, though some of his guests would bring their own. Particularly Somersby, who could expound on the merits of a good hunting weapon for hours at a time.

"Reginald." Gabriel's steward would be hovering just outside his study about now, no doubt hoping that Gabriel would ring for tea or some such nonsense.

"Yes, my lord," the older man replied, stepping into the study almost immediately. His thinning black hair showed far more gray than black at his temples, and he had a long, narrow face and prominent nose. He wore the dignity of an earl's steward like a shield.

"Make sure to seat Somersby at the other end of the table at dinner during the house party. I want to enjoy these last two weeks." Gabriel sat at his desk and opened his correspondence.

"Then why did you invite him, my lord?"

"Impertinent," Gabriel groused halfheartedly. He didn't give a whit what Reginald asked. The man had been the Hawthorne family steward for over two decades. Were he ever to fire the cantankerous old fatwit, he'd likely lose more than half of his staff for the effort. "I'm hoping he'll be my proxy in Parliament. A man can only stand so much posturing and ridiculous debate, but Somersby seems to relish it."

"Little wonder," Reginald muttered. Then louder, "Are we also expecting Lady Montrose?"

"No. We've ended our arrangement."

"Very good, my lord." Reginald's tone brightened considerably with that news. Apparently, Gabriel wasn't the only man disenchanted with the voluptuous widow.

"You still plan to leave for London on All Saints' Day?" the steward inquired.

He grimaced at the thought. "Or the following. Is everything ready for my guests' arrival?"

Reginald huffed. "Yes, my lord. The rooms are aired, and Cook is already preparing menus."

"Thank you, Reginald."

Dismissed, the man left the study.

Gabriel relaxed back in his chair and smiled. His guests would arrive in two days' time for what he hoped would be an enjoyable house party. Besides plans for hunting and shooting, he had planned card games, and a musicale for the ladies, all culminating in a masquerade ball. He could have done without the last, but his sister Violet had begged and pleaded for it. He'd relented simply to make her happy.

Regardless, this was his last respite before journeying back to London for another God-awful Season. Even if he could secure a proxy for Parliament, the next eight months were going to be his own version of hell. Endless invitations to dinners and balls, simpering chits and their money-hungry mothers who hovered about him looking for weakness so they could pounce. A parade of suitors for Violet's hand in marriage.

Gabriel's stomach sank, and his chest felt heavy. She was of age, he reminded himself. After coming out last Season, young bucks had relentlessly pursued her until Gabriel had insisted on attending every event as her chaperone. Violet had not been happy. To this day, she bemoaned how many of her friends were already married. Gabriel no longer had an excuse. He would find a suitable match for Violet, even though it meant she would leave to live with her husband. The Season would begin soon enough. Until then, he had one last respite, and he intended to enjoy every moment of his freedom.

No sooner had the thought crossed his mind when a ruckus of banging doors and loud voices sounded from the entry hall. Gabriel rose and strode out of his study. From the top of the stairs, he could see Violet and Reginald practically yelling at one another while one of his footmen held a limp person in his arms. His housekeeper and a maid hovered around them.

"Violet, please tell me you didn't kill someone while out shopping today," he said as he descended into the chaos.

His sister rounded on him and put her hands on her hips. Her amber eyes flashed. Her green bonnet was askew, and water dripped from her limp, dark brown curls. When had it started to rain? "Of course not. I'd save that honor for someone I knew."

The way she stated it implied he might hold that honor in the future.

"Did the milliner have a sale on strangers, then?"

Violet huffed as he reached her side. "She stepped out in front of the carriage. We didn't run her down, but she took quite a fall."

"She's sleeping again," the footman added.

She? "Why did you bring her here?" he asked as he leaned closer to have a look at the woman in the footman's arms. Long, brown hair was plastered to her head so he couldn't see much of her face. Her skin was pale, and he glimpsed soft, pink lips. A few freckles dotted her nose and the cheek he could see.

"Should I have left her in the street after nearly running her over? Is that proper etiquette for these situations? I don't recall reading about that in *The Mirror of Graces*."

Gabriel shot her a dark look, then turned his attention back to their unexpected guest.

The footman adjusted her in his arms. "Seems she has a head injury, my lord."

"Oh?"

"Oy, she's bled on me good."

Now that the man mentioned it, Gabriel detected a faint coppery scent in the air. He closed his eyes for a moment, summoning patience before he turned back to Violet.

"I sent for the doctor already," she blurted. "We should settle her someplace warm."

"The drawing room," Gabriel ground out and followed behind the small party.

They lay the woman on a chaise lounge, and Violet tucked a pillow under her head. They hadn't used the drawing room much today and, as a result, there was a chill in the air. Gabriel set to stoking the fire.

"Someone get her a blanket," he said as he returned to the chaise and looked down at the woman. Now that her hair had been pushed off her face, he could see that she had delicate features. Pale skin and those pretty, pink lips. She wore tortoiseshell spectacles. He wondered what color her eyes were as he scanned the rest of her body. She wasn't tall, that was certain. She wore a thin, black shirt with capped sleeves. The wet material clung to her form, outlining every luscious inch of her breasts. He swallowed and dragged his gaze away, only to startle at her legs.

"Good God, are those trousers?"

Violet grinned, eyes shining with undisguised glee. "Scandalous, isn't it? I think we'll be the best of friends."

Gabriel tilted his head back and looked at the plaster ceiling with its intricate carvings. "Violet…"

"She needs our help, Gabriel."

"And we shall give it to her. The doctor is on the way?"

His sister nodded.

Good. With the jostling of her as they settled on the chaise, the woman should have roused. He noted the rise and fall of her chest as she drew steady breaths, the damp fabric stretching tightly with every move. Where the hell was that blanket? The next county over?

Before he could inquire, her eyes fluttered open. His heart thudded at the sight. Her eyes, framed by thick, dark lashes, were the most unusual shade, somewhere between blue and green.

She blinked and raised a hand to run her fingertips over his stubbled jaw. A slight smile teased her lips, and she hummed.

Gabriel cleared his throat and stepped back to keep a respectable distance between them. She latched onto his hand instead, her cool fingers wrapping around his palm. When he looked into her eyes again, they were clouded with pain and appeared unfocused. He didn't have the heart to tug his hand away. She seemed to need the comfort.

Violet put her hand on his arm, drawing his attention. "Thank you, Gabriel. I know we have guests arriving, but she looked so lost when I tried to help her."

"You spoke to her?" Violet nodded. "What did she say?"

"Nothing. She seemed disoriented, so I brought her here. Looking like she does, I wasn't sure…"

If anyone else would help her. The words, though unspoken, rang true. A woman wearing trousers was likely to find the wrong attention, even in a small village like Marston.

"You did well, Vi."

She beamed at him and wrapped her arms around his waist. "She won't be any trouble, I promise."

Gabriel glanced back at the woman. Somehow, he doubted that. Especially with Violet around. As much as he loved his sister, she was willful, mischievous, and often drove him mad. God help him if there were two women like that living under his roof.

"When do people arrive?" Violet asked, dragging him out of his thoughts.

"Thursday."

"Will Christian be here?"

"By God, he better, or I'll drag him out of his house myself." Gabriel had written to the man three times about it. With every year that passed, Christian retreated further from society. Even country house parties like this one. It didn't matter that he'd become the Earl of Huntington. So long as someone else could see to his estates, Christian was happy to spend hours in his workshop with his gadgets. They'd been friends for over a decade and a half, since schooling at Eton. Gabriel had no intention of letting the man become a complete recluse. If he had to suffer through a Season, then he'd make damn sure that Christian was right there to suffer with him. It's what friends did.

Violet giggled. "I'm awfully glad that you're not my best friend, Gabriel."

"As am I, Vi." He said the words but didn't mean them. In his heart, he knew he'd miss Violet terribly when she wed and moved away. Perhaps he could wait a little longer to find her a suitable match. It was selfish of him, but he couldn't regret the thought. The house would be too quiet without her.

A carriage pulled into the drive then, the clip clop of the horse's hooves muted by the windows and light rain.

"That'll be the doctor," Reginald said.

Gabriel nodded. "Show him in."

Chapter Two

LILY HAD THE worst headache of her life. Too much movement made her head spin and her stomach churn. She lay on a couch of some sort surrounded by people and tried to take steady breaths. Slowly, her vision cleared.

A pretty young woman with dark curls tucked a blanket around her. "There you are. Nice and warm."

She hadn't realized she was cold until that moment. How did her clothes get wet? Lily tried to think through the throbbing pain. She remembered being at her apartment and a bright light. Then a horse and a bellhop. The rest was a blur.

Another voice joined those around her, but Lily couldn't quite focus. She lifted her hand, intending to touch the back of her head where the throbbing was most painful and was startled to realize she was holding someone's hand. A strong, masculine hand, with neatly trimmed fingernails. She followed the line of his hand, up the arm wearing a long sleeve shirt, over a wide shoulder, and up to a face that made her breath catch.

He had to be one of the most gorgeous men she'd ever seen. Thick black hair with strands of deep brown framed a strong face with high cheekbones, a straight nose, and firm lips. His chin had a bit of stubble she found incredibly appealing, and when he looked down at her, she stared into eyes of deep green with a ring of golden brown in the center. Lily had always loved hazel eyes, and the intensity she saw in their depths made her want to keep staring. Movie-star-handsome was too bland a description.

His thumb stroked over the back of her knuckles, reminding her that she held his hand. Lily looked at their joined hands again. The solid strength in his grip seemed to settle her nerves. Helped her gather more of her scattered thoughts. She squeezed his hand lightly and absorbed the comfort that small connection provided.

Another man knelt beside her, then. He had a shock of gray hair, ruddy cheeks, and faded blue eyes behind wire-rimmed glasses. He wore a dark brown coat over a shirt with some sort of fussy tie. He looked like an old railroad baron that had fallen on hard times. "Well, now. What have we here? Took a fall, did you?"

Had she? She gently touched the back of her head with her free hand and felt a wet lump. She remembered now. She fell back in her chair at her apartment and hit her head on the bookshelf. Then she'd fallen in the street. Wait, how did she get into the street?

The elderly man moved her hand aside and gently prodded her bump.

Lily hissed and nausea swamped her. She swallowed several times. "Ow."

"Did she pass out?" the man asked as he withdrew his hands and wiped them on a handkerchief. Brown smudges marred the white cloth.

Blood. The wetness she felt had been blood, at least in part.

"Yes, for a few minutes," the woman with the brown curls said.

Lily looked at her again. The woman was younger than Lily by at least five or six years. She couldn't have been more than twenty. She had bright amber eyes and creamy pale skin and wore a green gown with a high waist and lace trim that looked like something out of the Regency period. For that matter, the railroad baron, whom she now realized was actually a doctor, could fit into that time period with his clothes. Behind them, Lily spotted a room with light yellow paint and formal, antique furniture. "Where am I?"

"Never mind that," the railroad baron said. "Do you see stars about your eyes? Feel sickly in your stomach?"

Lily nodded and immediately groaned and pressed a hand to her forehead. Her vision swam and her stomach revolted again.

"A concussion from the bump to the head. Give her laudanum for the pain and nausea. It will help—"

Laudanum? That was something she read about in her romance novels. She'd never heard the term used in real life. Didn't...didn't laudanum have opium in it? Or was made from opiates? Either way, she didn't want it.

Before she could respond, the strong man holding her hand spoke. "No laudanum."

"Lord Rothden..." the doctor said.

"No." He nearly growled the word at the elderly man. "I will not allow laudanum to be used in this house."

"As you wish. She will need to rest for a few days until the dizziness and nausea fades. I daresay a warm bath will soothe her pain. She's likely to have some bruises as well." The doctor stood and stuffed his handkerchief into his pocket. "If she falls unconscious again, send for me immediately."

"We shall," the woman said.

"Lord Rothden. Lady Violet." The doctor bowed and left the room.

Lord and Lady? Now that the doctor wasn't blocking her view, she could see that the room they were in was huge with large windows that let in the last of the fading sunlight. The furniture was ornate and covered in patterned brocades and silks. It was the kind of room she'd expect to see in a historical home that gave tours. Something clicked. Lord and Lady. They must be historical reenactment actors. Of course. She let out a breath of relief.

"We can't put her there, Gabriel," the woman whispered. "She's not a servant."

"The guest rooms will be full in two days' time. I doubt your charge will be well enough by then."

"Not entirely full. Didn't you say that Lady Montrose wasn't attending?"

Lily saw the woman cross her arms and smile triumphantly.

Green-gold eyes met Lily's. The man brushed his thumb over her knuckles, then nodded. "I'll carry her up."

He bent and scooped Lily into his arms.

She squealed in surprise and grabbed his wide shoulders. Holy cow, they felt like solid muscle under his shirt. She ran one hand over his shoulder, feeling the hard warmth, and breathed in his scent. He smelled amazing, like pine and musk.

He made a noise in the back of his throat, and she snatched her hand back.

Don't pet the hot guy, Lily! Men like him didn't look twice at a woman like her. She'd learned that bitter lesson with her last boyfriend.

She pushed her glasses up her nose. "I can walk." He was strong, but Lily wasn't exactly tall and willowy. She had an hourglass figure that she liked, but she'd never been carried by anyone.

He didn't jostle her at all as he strode out of the room and started up a grand staircase. "Don't be ridiculous. I'll not allow you to walk up the stairs with a head injury."

He had a delicious voice that was a bit husky.

"Who-who are you?"

"Rothden. And this is my sister, Lady Violet."

"Rothden is an unusual name. I've never heard it before."

Lily saw a flicker of surprise cross his face.

"It's a family name."

He sounded so formal when he spoke. What did he sound like when he wasn't in character?

"I'm Lily. Lily Bennett."

"Are you American?" Violet asked from behind them as they climbed the stairs.

"Er...yes?" It struck Lily then that Rothden and Violet had very good English accents. She wondered if they were real. It made sense to hire English actors for a quality re-enactment. Especially in a grand home like this.

"How delightful! I've only ever met one American before. I'd love to go there. Rothden, you will have to allow me a husband who will take me to America."

Rothden slanted a look over his shoulder as he stepped onto the landing of the third floor. "We are not discussing this until we get to London."

Violet made a face at his back, and Lily bit back a smile. She also caught Rothden's mistake. Lady Violet talked about going to America, but he just mentioned going to London. They must be close to Corbin, because London wasn't far away. It took only ten minutes to drive from Bookhalla to the restaurant in London when she'd dropped off the contract to Mr. Samuel.

She needed to call her boss at the first opportunity to let him know of her injury and ask for tomorrow off. Maybe she should call Bellamy, too. Although, if she were home in a day or two, Bells probably wouldn't even know she'd been gone. They weren't close. Hadn't been since their parents died.

God, the only person she had to call when she needed help was an old man who hired her out of pity. Her heart twisted in her chest as the thought sank in. Lily felt very alone.

Rothden carried her down a long hallway and stopped before a wood-paneled door. Violet held it open while he carried Lily into a bedroom three times the size of her efficiency apartment.

The walls were painted a lovely light green with white paneling along the bottom. A chaise and a couple chairs sat near a fireplace, and paintings of colorful landscapes hung on the walls. The four-poster bed was made of intricately carved wood, with a coverlet and curtains that matched the walls. She even spotted a changing screen in the corner. Every detail of a nineteenth-century home, exactly as she'd pictured dozens of times while reading her favorite romances.

Rothden carried her through the room and laid her gently on the bed.

Their gazes met. He swept a lock of hair off her cheek and tucked it behind her ear. Lily got another whiff of his delicious scent before he released her and stepped back. "I'll call for a bath," he said. "Vi, will you arrange something more suitable for her to wear?"

"Of course. I'll sit with her."

A hot bath sounded like heaven. The aches in her body were beginning to make themselves known, and she felt like she'd been rolling in the mud. Lily looked at her jeans. They were dirty, and there was a rip in one knee. Her tee shirt didn't look any better.

With a start, she was getting the beautiful bed dirty. She scrambled off the thick mattress. Which proved to be a mistake. Her head spun and her legs went out from under her.

Strong hands caught her before she hit the floor.

Rothden scooped her up and put her back in bed. "Are you trying to reinjure yourself?"

"I'm getting your clean sheets dirty!"

"They can be cleaned."

"I'm at least taking my shoes off." She reached for her tennis shoes and winced.

He sighed and reached for her shoe. His hand froze and he stared at her foot.

Lily looked down. She wore a pair of black Converses she'd found at a second-hand store a couple weeks ago. She'd always wanted a pair of Chucks when she was in high school but hadn't been able to afford them. Especially when she'd spent every penny she earned on bills and food while raising Bellamy.

"You have corsets on your shoes," Violet said with excitement. "American fashion is quite different, isn't it? It would be positively scandalous for a woman to wear breeches here." Violet tilted her head to look at Lily's pants. Her eyes glowed with interest, and Lily could practically see the desire to put them on.

Rothden pinched the bridge of his nose. "Suitable clothing, Vi. For *England*. I'll send the maid up." He took one last look at Lily, then left and shut the door behind him.

Lily watched him leave. God, he looked just as good from the back as he did the front. He was tall, with those wide shoulders and narrow waist. With that thick dark hair and those hazel eyes, he was every woman's fantasy. Even if he never looked twice at her, she could dream, right?

When she turned back to Violet, the young woman had a slight smile on her lips. "My brother is exceedingly handsome, isn't he?"

Lily pushed up her glasses and hoped she wasn't flushed scarlet. "He must have women lining up around the block."

Violet laughed. "And their mothers. He's avoided the marriage mart admirably though." She paused, then added, "I should like to see him happily settled down. Since taking over the estate, he's lost much of the humor he once had. He spends most of his time in his study over the accounts, and when we're in Town, he is either hanging over me as a chaperone or keeping as much distance as possible from the young ladies looking for a husband."

"Sounds as if he doesn't want a wife."

"What he wants and what he needs are two different things," Violet said with a sniff.

Lily grinned. Then her smile slipped as she thought of Archer. Something terrible had happened to her brother on his last tour. Something that damaged him on the inside far more than his physical injuries. Maybe if she bought that cabin, he could come stay with her for a while. She needed to check her email to see if the realtor had responded. Unfortunately, she didn't have her phone. She hoped it was in her apartment instead of out on the street where she'd fallen.

"I should call my sister. And my boss. Can I use your phone?"

"You are so worldly. Speaking terms I've never heard before. I wish I could travel." Violet flushed a bit. "I don't know what a phone is, so I don't think we have one. If you want to write a note, we shall have it dispatched to them."

"When do you get off of work, Violet?" The formal routine was lovely, but she really needed to call her boss at the least.

Violet blinked. "Oh, I'm not part of the working class. Are you?"

"Sure. I work in a bookstore in Corbin."

"How terribly exciting."

It should have been. Lily ignored the emptiness that crept in every time she thought of her job. Once she found a house, and Lily and Archer visited more often, then everything would be better. Even her job. It had to be.

"Can I use your computer?" Lily asked. "I'll just send them a quick email. Let everyone know that I'm okay."

Violet shook her head, her brows drawn together.

She genuinely looked like she didn't understand what Lily was talking about. Damn, she was a really good actress.

There was a soft scratch at the door, then it opened to half a dozen people.

Lily's mouth dropped open as two men carried in a bathtub and set it near the fire. Maids followed and dumped pails of steaming water into the tub.

"One of the maids will help you undress while I fetch a nightgown for you. I'll have a tray sent up for our supper." Violet took Lily's hand and gave it a gentle squeeze.

A nagging feeling of unease hit her. She touched a hand to the back of her head and felt the lump. The room with its antique furniture, the

English accents, and the bath, even the clothing…if this was a re-enactment, it was a very good one. The no-expense-spared kind.

Violet said something to one of the women wearing a drab brown gown with a white apron and then left, following the others out and closing the door.

The maid gave Lily a small curtsey. "May I help you undress, Miss?"

"Uh…"

The woman looked down at Lily's shoes. "Oy, your shoes have corset ties!"

The feeling of unease turned into fear as another thought struck Lily. What if this wasn't a re-enactment? It was too straightforward to be a dream.

What if I'm in a coma?

GABRIEL SAT BACK in his chair and rubbed his eyes. He'd been working on the estate accounts for hours, trying to make sure all was in order before his guests arrived. He'd checked that last column three times and ended with three different sums. Nothing for it. He'd have to come back to them tomorrow.

He stretched his tired limbs, then snuffed out the candle on his desk and rose. The clock in the hall chimed twelve as he left his study and climbed the stairs. His thoughts turned once more to the young woman in the bedchamber next to his. Gabriel had found himself thinking of her quite often as he'd worked tonight. Everything about her was unusual. Her clothes, her shoes, her speech, even her spectacles were unlike anything he'd ever seen before. The few people he'd met from the colonies were different in their own way, much like peers from the continent. None were like Miss Bennett. He couldn't quite determine which social class she belonged to. Her clothing suggested the lower class, and yet…Gabriel shook his head. The woman was a mystery. He rubbed his eyes, too tired to consider it further tonight.

As he approached his bedchamber, a narrow band of light under the door next to his drew his gaze. He stopped outside Miss Bennett's door. He heard a soft snore. Ah, no doubt someone left a candle lit or the fireplace hadn't burned down to coals yet.

Gabriel took a step toward his chamber when another sound made him pause. He leaned closer. Was that a sniffle? He heard the slight clearing of a feminine throat, followed by another snore. Before he realized his intentions, he knocked lightly on the chamber door.

"Uh… hello?"

"Miss Bennett? Are you well?" he called. This was entirely inappropriate, but the gentleman in him didn't seem to care a whit.

The door opened, and Gabriel's heart thumped in his chest. Miss Bennett stood in a thin night rail with her golden-brown curls in a wild, thick mass about her shoulders. Her eyes were tinged a bit red behind her spectacles and looked glossy in the dim light.

Violet sprawled in a chair by the bed, asleep.

"Is something amiss, Miss Bennett?"

She shook her head. Then nodded. Her shoulders sagged, and she wandered toward the window.

Despite his better judgment, he stepped into the room. With Violet asleep, Miss Bennett was technically unchaperoned. Although, for all he knew of her, she could be married.

She drew back the curtain and waved at the darkness beyond the windowpane. "Where are the airplanes? Where are the power lines? The cars? Why aren't there any light switches in this room? Where is the *toilet*? I had to use a chamber pot earlier! I get re-enactment, but there are still some conveniences of the modern age, even if they're hidden." Her voice rose as she spoke, and emotion clogged her throat.

Gabriel studied her. None of the words she seemed to be inquiring about were familiar to him. "Are those things you would find in the colonies?"

She blew out a breath. "Yes. But even if we were in England, which we can't be, then there would still be a freaking car or a power line."

Was she mad? Perhaps she needed one of those hospitals for the mentally incompetent. "Why can't we be in England?"

Miss Bennett rolled her eyes in the same way Vi often did when he said something she thought was ridiculous. "I was knocked out when I hit my head. People don't tend to get on airplanes when they're unconscious." Whatever she saw in his expression made her cross her arms over her ample bosom.

Gabriel realized he was staring and yanked his gaze back up to her face.

"I'll prove it. What is the date today?" she asked.

"The nineteenth of October."

"Well, there you go."

"I don't follow." Actually, he didn't follow most of this conversation. He'd have to send for Doctor Wells again. His guests would arrive the day after tomorrow. He couldn't have a mad woman in his home.

"I arrived here, wherever *here* is, just before dark so I couldn't have been out for more than twenty minutes. You can't cross the Atlantic in that short of time, no matter how fast the plane is. We're still in Kentucky. Not England."

"Miss Bennett, I have no idea what a plane is, but I can assure you that we are in England. I think perhaps you should rest. Maybe with some sleep, all will sort itself out in—"

She growled and stomped toward him. Those unusual blue-green eyes glittered. Then she grabbed his shirt in her small fists and shook him. "Stop with the re-enactment. You're making me feel like I'm crazy."

Feminine heat washed over him at her nearness, and he smelled the light floral scent of her skin from the bath. His cock stiffened. *Good Christ, Rothden. Not now.* Gabriel covered her hands in his. "Miss Bennett."

"Lily."

"*Miss Bennett.* You've had a difficult day. A night of good sleep will certainly make everything better tomorrow."

"Please. Just tell me that in the morning I will see cars and power lines and planes, and I will go to bed." Her fingers dug into his shirt, holding him close. *"Please."*

She beseeched him so earnestly that it tugged at him. Despite the words she spoke and her odd behavior, he couldn't quite convince himself that she was disturbed. But he couldn't give her his word on something he didn't understand. "I can't."

Her shoulders slumped, and she rested her forehead on his chest.

Gabriel sucked in a breath. He looked down at her mass of curls against the white of his shirt. Miss Bennett was on the shorter side. The top of her head just reached his shoulders.

"I'm in a coma," she mumbled against his chest.

"I'm not of the medical profession, but I don't believe it is common for a comatose person to stand in a bedchamber and talk to others."

She lifted her head and met his gaze.

Gabriel saw real fear there. Her skin paled, and her fingers shook where they still gripped his shirt. Everything in him stilled. Narrowed down to the trembling woman. He wrapped his arms around her slim form and pulled her against his chest. He *needed* to comfort her. The compulsion was so strong, he could scant think of anything else.

She relaxed into his embrace, wrapped her arms around his waist, and laid her head over his heart. Her breasts pressed against his chest, and a fresh curl of awareness moved through him. Gabriel rubbed a hand over her back as he would when comforting Violet, but nothing about Miss Bennett felt sisterly. Every warm breath skating over his chest tightened his gut and made his heart beat faster.

He held her until her trembling stopped, and she drew a deep breath.

She stepped back but didn't release him. "Thank you," she whispered. "I'm sorry for freaking out on you. You don't even know me, and I just plastered myself against you."

Her cheeks flushed, and she ducked her head.

Gabriel put a finger under her chin and lifted it until she met his gaze. "Worry not, Miss Bennett."

Her lips curled in a slight smile. Then she rose on her toes and pressed a kiss to his cheek.

The scent of her, like the roses of her bath and a deeper fragrance that was all her, washed over him until it filled every breath he took.

"You're right. Everything will be better tomorrow after I've had some sleep." She pushed several curls out of her face and tucked them behind her ear.

Gabriel wanted to touch the silk strands. To wrap them in his fist and breathe her in. He stepped back before he acted like a besotted fool. He forced himself to cross the room and wake Violet.

His sister mumbled something, then shook her head. "Wha…?"

"It's late, Vi. Go find your bed. Miss Bennett will be fine until morning."

Violet blinked several times until she spotted their guest.

"Thank you for staying," Miss Bennett said. "I'll be okay."

He helped Vi to her feet and steered her toward the door. At the threshold, he glanced back. Miss Bennett had removed her spectacles and set them on the table beside the bed. She looked different but no less lovely. "Goodnight, Miss Bennett."

"Goodnight, Rothden."

Gabriel closed the door behind him. At the threshold, he wrapped an arm around Vi's shoulders and pressed a kiss to her temple.

She murmured "good night" and shuffled into the room.

Once she was safely tucked inside, he sought his own bed. As he closed his eyes, thoughts of their guest filled his thoughts. He didn't understand his reaction to her. Certainly, he'd been with women more beautiful and cultured. Caroline, his last lover, was lauded as one of the most beautiful women in the country. Yet she had never stirred these strange feelings in him. He didn't like it. Miss Bennett already disturbed the peace he needed in the last weeks before making the journey to Town for the Season. If he had any hope of true respite, she had to go.

CHAPTER THREE

LILY ADJUSTED THE bodice of her gown, shifting it a bit so she could breathe. Since her own clothes were ripped and dirty, she'd had to borrow something from Violet. And apparently, the woman's entire wardrobe consisted of Regency-era dresses. The white gown she'd borrowed was pretty, with an empire waist, puffy sleeves, and a pink ribbon that ran under the breasts. Boobs that were currently squeezed into a gown that was a little too snug. Compared to Violet, she was quite a bit more well-endowed. Her breasts pushed against the low, square neckline, and the sheer scarf thing they added to the top kept them from spilling out.

"It looks far better on you than it does on me," Violet said. The young woman had arrived with an armload of dresses and undergarments shortly after Lily woke. Even slippers. Thankfully, they wore close to the same size shoe.

"I doubt that," Lily said, shifting the dress again.

Violet grabbed her hands and pulled them away. "We'll ask Ga—Rothden. He'll tell us who looks better in it. Now let's go down to breakfast. I'm hungry."

Lily nodded. Thankfully, the terrible headache from yesterday had subsided to a dull throb, and the knot on the back of her head wasn't as tender. She still had moments of dizziness, but they weren't quite as often.

She let Violet lead her out of the room and down the stairs. Heat flooded her cheeks when she thought of her late-night visit from Rothden. She'd had a freaking meltdown in the arms of the most gorgeous man she'd ever seen. Clung to him like she could crawl inside his skin. She pressed her hands to her hot cheeks. How mortifying.

Hot guys don't look at women like you, remember Lily?

They wanted women like Bellamy. A lifetime of being overlooked had taught her that. Violet's brother had just been being kind. She tried not to remember how good it felt when he held her, or how good he'd smelled.

Rothden had thick, black hair threaded with dark brown that brushed his collar and those hazel green eyes that glinted more gold when he looked at her. High cheekbones and lips women probably fantasized about kissing, along with that shadow of stubble… Lily nearly groaned. Why did she have to be attracted to the most unattainable men on the planet? She paused on the last step when they reached the entry hall. He'd probably trip over his tongue if he saw Bellamy.

Lily stomped on the curl of jealousy forming in her gut. She might not be gorgeous, but she was pretty enough and her figure was good. She glanced down at the top of her boobs which were accentuated by the borrowed gown. Some men found that attractive. And maybe she didn't have an amazing job like Bellamy or a military career like Archer, but she would. Eventually. Just as soon as she found a place to call home. Then she could figure out what she wanted to do. Hopefully, she could even find a nice guy at some point who wouldn't cheat on her or try to turn her into a shorter version of her supermodel sister.

"Miss Bennett?" Violet called.

Lily's head snapped up, and she realized that she was still on the last step. Violet stood in the doorway of another room, eyebrows raised.

"Sorry. I…" *was just wishing that I was as beautiful as my sister so that your brother would look my way.* Gah, she was losing her mind.

"It's all right. Everyone's entitled to a bit of wool-gathering."

Lily joined her and smiled. She liked Violet. The younger woman was bright and funny, and her eyes seemed to sparkle with delight at the smallest of things. "Please, call me Lily."

"Only if you will call me Violet."

Lily smiled. "Agreed."

They entered a large dining room with a table that easily sat twelve. Sunlight shone brightly through the windows, making the room feel cheery. A man in a suit and a woman in a drab brown gown with a white apron stood against one wall. Rothden sat at the head of the table with a newspaper in his hands, his breakfast half-eaten.

"Good morning, Brother," Violet said as she reached his side and planted a kiss on his cheek. "I managed to get our Miss Bennett out of bed and bring her down to breakfast. She is feeling much improved." Violet gave her a wink, then turned to the food set out on the sideboard.

It smelled like eggs and sausage and toast. Lily's stomach growled.

Rothden lowered the newspaper and their gazes met. His hazel eyes swept over her dress, lingered, then rose to her face.

Lily gave him a small wave. Then mentally smacked herself. *Be an adult and use some words, why don't you?* Ugh.

"Good morning," she said. "Thank you. For everything."

Rothden rose from his chair. "You're looking well. The gown is lovely."

"Doesn't it look better on her than on me?" Violet asked as she piled her plate high with food.

Rothden swept his gaze over her once more. She couldn't quite read the look in his eyes.

"The dress compliments you, Miss Bennett. I'm glad that my sister could loan you something suitable."

Lily tried not to be disappointed that he didn't answer Violet's question. Or perhaps he had, by not agreeing.

He waved to the sideboard. "Please, have some breakfast and join us."

Lily took a China plate with a pink and blue floral pattern and focused on food. Violet had had a tray of food sent up to Lily's room for dinner last night, and they'd shared a bit, but she hadn't had much of an appetite. She was quite hungry this morning.

Violet sat beside Rothden, telling him something about a visit to a store and a woman she thought was rude. He made non-verbal sounds at the right intervals, but Lily didn't think he was really listening.

When she joined them, he stood and held out her chair. The serving woman came over to pour some tea into a cup, then returned to her position against the wall. Lily smiled at both and dug into her food. It was odd though. There were no tourists here, but Violet and Rothden, even the servers acted as if they were really in the Regency era. They weren't using modern conveniences. She'd had to use a chamber pot instead of a toilet. Who did that?

"Do you think Somersby will ask me to dance at the ball?" Violet asked, drawing Lily back to their conversation. "Should I have my slippers lined with lead?"

Rothden choked on his tea and set the cup aside. "I hardly think dancing with him calls for such drastic preparation."

"He didn't step on *your* feet. I don't think the idea is so unreasonable."

Rothden heaved a sigh. "Perhaps you shouldn't dance with any of them."

Lily hid a smile. How often had Archer given that same sigh to her or Bellamy? Thoughts of her brother made the smile dissolve. He still wasn't returning her calls. She silently cursed him, even as her worry shot up another notch.

"You don't want me to like any of your friends. You're afraid one of them might offer for me, is that it?" Violet asked.

Rothden slapped the newspaper down on Lily's side of the table. "None of my friends are worthy of you. I'd rather—"

Lily's gaze snagged on the newspaper as the siblings began to bicker. She leaned forward. The story on the front said something about a coalition with Napoleon. She pulled the paper closer and pushed her glasses up. In the corner, the date read 20 October 1813.

She blinked. The date didn't change to one that made more sense. She glanced around the room, noting the wall by the door and the chandelier full of candles overhead. Her breath froze in her lungs.

Lily shot to her feet, almost tipping her chair over.

Rothden and Violet stopped arguing and looked at her.

She rushed out of the room, through the entry hall, and yanked open the front door, then dashed down the stairs to the gravel drive. She spun in a slow circle. Dizziness swamped her, but she fought it back. There wasn't a car in sight. Nothing but pretty gardens, and farther down the drive, trees. No asphalt parking lots for visitors or signs for bus parking. No power lines going to the house. No light switches, toilets, or light bulbs.

She started breathing fast but couldn't draw a full breath.

Rothden appeared in the doorway and ran down the steps toward her. "Miss Bennett, are you well?"

She fluttered her hands, feeling like an elephant was standing on her chest.

He took hold of her upper arms. Whatever he saw in her eyes made him tug her against his chest.

Lily wrapped her arms around his waist and held tight. Right now, she needed the comfort of Rothden's arms. It was crazy, because she didn't know him at all, but when he held her, she felt safe. She'd feel bad later about falling apart on him again.

Because she wasn't in a coma. She'd tasted the delicious food.

Smelled Rothden's clean scent. Oh God, he smelled so good. She'd heard the clink of the silver spoon against her China cup and felt the strength in Rothden's arms as he held her. It was all too real. Too visceral.

"What year is it?" she asked.

He stilled. "It is 1813."

How was it possible? She couldn't have time traveled. That wasn't real, was it?

Rothden rubbed a large palm on her back. "Miss Bennett?"

She lifted her head from his chest.

A clattering of hooves on the drive made them turn. A black carriage pulled by a single horse approached and stopped a few feet away. A man in navy blue livery exited the house and opened the door of the carriage. The doctor stepped out, and when he saw them, tipped his hat.

"I didn't expect to see you on your feet quite so soon," the older man said.

"What year is it?" Lily demanded.

Bushy silver eyebrows rose over his faded eyes. "It's 1813." He glanced at Rothden and then back to Lily. "What year do you think it is?"

All sound faded except for the pounding of her heart. She saw the honest confusion on his face. The awful truth hit her. They weren't re-enactment actors. This wasn't Kentucky. Somehow, she'd done the impossible, and traveled back in time.

Images of her last moments in her apartment flooded to mind then. Heating up that awful frozen dinner that she never ate and fixing the little clock that looked like a Faberge egg. Watching the ballroom dancers come together as the clock struck the hour. And a blinding white light.

Lily gasped. It had to have been that clock. The dancers looked like a couple from the Regency period. If it was the clock, where was it now? Had she dropped it somewhere? Oh God. How would she get home?

"YOU'RE CERTAIN, DR. Wells?" Gabriel stood at the window in the library, watching Miss Bennett and Violet stroll through the gardens beyond. Miss Bennett stared into the distance while Violet chattered on about something. He and the doctor had moved to the library to talk privately after Miss Bennett's episode in the driveway. The woman had panicked when they told her the year. Even stranger, she thought she was from some distant time in the future. Impossible, of course. She must be mad.

The chair creaked as Wells shifted in it. He sat facing the fire with a wool blanket over his lap. "As certain as I can be, my lord. I've treated many concussions and the signs tend to be the same. Further, her eyes are clear and her thoughts are coherent, even if the things she is saying are…"

"Mad?" Gabriel supplied as he faced the man.

The doctor adjusted his wire-frame spectacles, and his ruddy cheeks darkened. "If one takes a strictly logical approach to the world."

"As a man of science, I expected that would be your view."

"What we consider science and healing were once thought to be magic by our forbearers. Who is to say that the things we believe to be impossible are not achievable in some distant future? Regardless, the young woman believes that she is from another time. Whether she is or not, who can say? Of a certainty, her manner of dress and speech are not from the village."

"Even those of my acquaintance from America do not sound or dress as she does," Gabriel admitted.

"My advice is unchanged. The young lady needs rest. Especially with this added stress of what year she finds herself in." He paused, studying the flickering flames. "My lord, I do not impose this upon you, but in my estimation, the lady has nothing. None of her own clothing or shoes. No family or friends that we are aware of. If you found yourself in an unknown place with not a shred to your person, would you not also panic?"

Gabriel considered the man's words. Likely he would find himself uncomfortable with such a situation. "It is my duty to help those in my care. Rest assured doctor, that I provide for what is mine. I do not know how to help her with this business of traveling from the future, but perhaps in time, her mind will provide some answer."

"Very good." A glimmer of approval shone on the man's face. "I feel that I leave her in good hands."

The thought of Miss Bennett's silken skin under his hands had heat curling in his gut. Gabriel clenched his teeth and forced the image from his mind. "Thank you, Dr. Wells. We shall call for you if we need anything further."

The elderly man rose from the chair and lay the blanket aside. He patted his thick white hair as if looking for his hat, then looked around for it. When it didn't appear, he gave a short nod. "Lord Rothden."

Reginald stepped into the library. No doubt his steward had been hovering outside, listening for the moment he could escort the doctor out. How the man managed the servants was a mystery when he seemed to spend his entire day lurking outside whatever room Gabriel happened to be in.

"If you will come with me, Dr. Wells, I will show you out." Reginald gave Gabriel a short bow, a lock of thinning black hair falling onto his narrow forehead, then said, "Shall I send Lady Violet in?"

Rothden found his gaze drawn back to the window. Miss Bennett had her hands crossed over her chest, no doubt fighting off the chill of autumn in her thin morning gown. He remembered the moment she'd entered the dining room wearing the borrowed frock, the dress clinging to her delectable figure. The flush of desire he'd felt startled him. He was a man who appreciated a nice bosom. Certainly, he wasn't feeling *attraction* to the lady. She wasn't the sort he usually spent his time with. He preferred taller women who didn't wear spectacles, for a start. Although her skin looked quite smooth. Would she feel soft—

Reginald cleared his throat loudly.

Blast. What had he asked? "Yes, please send Lady Violet up to my study."

"Yes, my lord." Reginald and the doctor quit the room.

His sister hadn't left Miss Bennett's side since her arrival yesterday afternoon. He'd never seen Violet so attentive to something or someone. With the exception of her focus of finding a husband. Gabriel sighed. He'd consider that prospect once they were in London and not a moment sooner. Besides, he had to finish the accounts before his guests arrived. He took one last, lingering look out the window at Miss Bennett, then left the library and took the stairs up to his study.

The faint restlessness inside him settled when he entered. Gabriel spent a great deal of time here when they weren't in London, so he'd made the room one of comfort. The walls were a light yellow and thick, blue velvet curtains covered the windows. He'd kept his father's ornate desk, but added a plush chair and some bookcases. Running the Rothden estate was a monumental task. As a young man, he knew he would one day become the Earl of Rothden. Only, he hadn't known it would be far sooner than he anticipated or that, when it came, the estate would be in financial hardship. He'd worked tirelessly to improve their fortunes, and now they were back to being some of the wealthiest in the Ton. A fact of which he was damn proud.

A few minutes later, Violet rapped softly on the door and stepped into his study. Her dark brown curls framed her oval face and sparkling amber eyes. She looked much like their mother, although with far more mischief in her smile. Thoughts of his mother soured his mood. He turned his mind to the upcoming party and their mysterious guest.

"It's quite chilly out this morn," Violet said. "I would have stayed in, but Lily—that is, our Miss Bennett—seemed in quite a state and wanted fresh air."

Gabriel sat at his desk with a stack of reports from his holdings and the estate books waiting for his attention. *Our* Miss Bennett, indeed. "What did she say?"

"Not much." Violet's nose scrunched, and she looked away.

"Nothing unusual?" he pressed. Violet couldn't lie worth a damn, but that didn't keep her from trying when she thought she could protect someone or get away with it.

"She did ask what year it was, but with the bump on her head…" Violet clasped her fingers together and walked forward to sit on the corner of his desk. "I'm certain with some rest, she'll be well soon."

"Violet."

"Anyone would be out of sorts after almost being run over by a carriage."

"*Violet.*"

"Gabriel," she huffed. Then, "She talked about the future."

"Ah. She told you she thought she was from some time in the distant future."

Violet ran her finger over the edge of his desk. "It might explain some of her odd mannerisms and clothing. Her shoes with the corset lacing, for one."

"I cannot fathom such a thing being true."

"But Gabriel, what if it were true? Wouldn't it be wondrous?"

Wondrous? "The lady would know nothing of living in our time. Everything would be foreign to her."

She laughed. "You should have heard her speak of using the chamber pot this morning. Or when I brought in gowns. She said she'd never worn so many layers in her life."

Gabriel tried not to think of Miss Bennett dressing. Or undressing. "I imagine it would be like arriving on some distant shore with not a shred to your name."

"What an exciting adventure that would be."

He shook his head. "Imagine her in Society, Violet. Regardless of where she came from, if she is unfamiliar with the stricter conventions many of the Ton seem to relish, the gossips will devour her." Good Christ, he could envision it now. He wouldn't let Miss Bennett anywhere near those shark-infested waters. Some of those old crones could smell blood.

Violet sat up straighter, eyes gleaming as she looked at him.

Gabriel nearly groaned. He was quite familiar with that expression. He held up a hand to stop whatever she meant to say, but Violet ignored him.

"Then we shall just have to teach her. What better time than with your house party, dear brother? Your friends will be far more relaxed than Society, and I daresay they will appreciate a new lady to dance with." She clapped her hands. "I can take her shopping. We can even find a ball gown for the masquerade. Won't it be exciting?"

Violet's grin was infectious. "You may have your fun, Vi. Find her some suitable gowns and whatever else she needs until we figure out where she comes from." A sudden thought occurred to him then. He frowned. "Vi, she's clearly of a marriageable age. What if she has a husband and children waiting for her somewhere?"

Her grin faded. Then her chin went up. "I shall find out. If she's a spinster, then we can be on the shelf together."

Gabriel narrowed his eyes.

Violet blew him a kiss.

"I will seriously consider suitors for you after we return to London," he ground out.

She grinned and hopped off of the desk in a swirl of white skirts. "I'll ask Reginald to have the carriage brought around and find a nice walking dress for Miss Bennett."

"I should like to speak with her before then."

Violet was halfway to the door when he spoke. She turned and gave him a look with which he was wholly unfamiliar. "I shall send her in."

CHAPTER FOUR

L ILY PACED HER bedroom, arms wrapped around her waist. Her breath had frozen in her lungs when the doctor confirmed what year it was, and she hadn't been able to draw a full breath since. Walking in the garden with Violet had helped calm her panic, but when the young woman had been called to Rothden's study, Lily realized how chilly it was and sought the warmth of the fire.

God, this was a mess. She'd traveled back in time. And when she'd accidentally blurted that out to Rothden and the doctor, their look of surprise was quickly overshadowed by a look that said, "This lady is nuts". Fortunately, Violet had emerged from inside and taken Lily to the lovely garden on the side of the house while Rothden and the doctor spoke privately.

She still wasn't convinced that they weren't going to lock her up. Mental facilities were bad during this time, weren't they? Lily couldn't remember. The only place like that she could think of was Bedlam, and it sounded like a hospital straight out of a horror flick.

Thankfully, Violet believed her. A grin tugged at her lips as she remembered their talk.

"Do you swear it's 1813?" Lily demanded as she and Violet stepped into the garden. Dark red dahlias flowered among the pretty white camellia bushes. Dots of pink and purple flowers twined with the fading rose bushes as the last blooms of summer faded. She gave it a passing glance, too wound up

to appreciate the beauty around her.

"Why would I lie about what year it is?" Violet asked. There was genuine confusion in her voice.

Lily covered her face with her hands and tried to breathe.

Violet took hold of her wrists and pulled her hands away. "What is it? Why the odd questions?"

God, she was afraid to tell Violet the truth. Rothden and the doctor were trying to decide what to do with her. "They're going to lock me up."

"Who is? Lock you where?"

She sighed and turned her hands over to clasp the younger woman's. Violet was a dreamer. That much was clear in just the few hours they'd spent together. She might be the only person that could keep the doctor from sending Lily to the nut house. But time travel was a stretch for anyone.

"I'm not from here, Violet."

"I gathered that by your odd clothing."

"Everyone wears jeans and tee shirts in my time. Violet, I'm..." here goes... "I'm from the future. Yesterday was October 19, 2022. Not 1813. Somehow I...traveled through time."

Violet squinted at her. "You mean to say that yesterday morning you were two hundred and nine years forward in time and by the afternoon, you found yourself here?"

"God, you did that math fast."

Violet gave a ladylike snort. "But that is what you're saying? That you come from a distant time?"

Lily nodded. Her breath stuck in her throat, afraid of what might come next. What if Violet didn't believe her either?

She shouldn't have worried.

After a moment of silence, Violet nodded. Then her eyes sparked and she squeezed Lily's hands. "You must tell me everything. What are the men like? Do you dance often? Oh, tell me all about America!"

"You believe me?"

"Of course. That's an oddly specific year to have picked if you were making the story up. Plus, you seemed genuinely panicked a few moments ago. Would you invent that as well?" Violet shrugged.

Lily threw her arms around Violet and hugged her. Not everyone thought she was crazy. She felt sure Violet would help her. She pulled out of the hug. "I know it sounds crazy, but it's true. I don't know how I got here, but I have to get home."

"It sounds like an adventure."

Lily smiled for the first time in what felt like hours. "I accidentally told Rothden and the doctor that I was from the future, and now they both think I'm crazy."

"Pish. My brother thinks I'm mad. Just because I dragged him out to this garden when I was ten to meet the king of the fairies. Of course, when we got back, the king was gone, so he thought I made it all up. Or the time I went through his purse looking for the shiniest silver coin to leave by the pond so I could draw the fairies back. He'd obviously scared them away with all of his bellowing about me being a silly child. I wanted them to come back so we could play."

Lily laughed. "Just don't let them commit me…"

She'd listened as Violet told her more adventures of growing up and tagging along behind Rothden and his friends. It made her think of Archer and Bellamy. What were they doing now? Would she know, even if she were back in her time? Lily sighed. She would figure out a way to get back home. She was going to buy that cabin, dammit, and they would be a family again. Violet and Rothden spoke to each other with affection, even when they'd bickered this morning. Lily missed that with her siblings.

I have to find a way to fix what is broken.

There was a light knock on her bedroom door. Lily opened it to an older man with thinning salt and pepper hair and wearing a dark suit without a single wrinkle.

"Miss Bennett, I am Reginald, Lord Rothden's steward. Lord Rothden asks me to bring you to his study, my lady."

"Oh, uh, thank you." Lily smoothed her hair back and tucked a stray curl behind her ear, adjusted the bodice of her dress, and followed the man down one flight of stairs to the second level. He had his arms clasped behind his back and walked with the authority of a king.

Rothden's study was not far down a hall paneled in dark wood with cream walls and several portraits of men and women in older fashions of dress. *Family ancestors?* she wondered.

The steward led her into a sunny room with a marble fireplace, and small seating area. Rothden sat behind an ornate desk, shuffling stacks of papers. With his thick hair and that appealing bit of stubble that shadowed his jaw, he made all of Lily's lady parts take notice.

Not for you, Lily.

Even if she wasn't two hundred years in the past, she couldn't have this handsome man any more than she could have a rock star like Mason, her last boyfriend. His band had been on the cusp of stardom. He spent time with her in private, but he never introduced her to his friends or his band mates. In the end, she realized that he hadn't wanted her at all.

"Miss Bennett," Reginald announced.

Rothden stood when she approached and motioned to one of the cushioned chairs in front of his desk. "Thank you for coming, Miss Bennett. Would you care to sit?"

Lily glanced back, but Reginald had left the room and closed the door behind him. She turned her attention back to her host but didn't sit. "I'm not crazy."

⟫⟫⟩⟨⟨⟨

THE TREMBLE IN her words shook him. As if their vibration carried through the air and into his body. He rounded the desk. "Miss Bennett, I can assure you that I have heard many a fantastic tale in my life. You *have* met my sister."

She gave a half laugh.

He reached out to touch her shoulders, then dropped his hands back to his sides. The need to offer her comfort warred with years of ingrained propriety.

"I doubt she's claimed she's from the year 2022."

"Nothing quite so specific." He smiled at her and watched the tension drain from her body. She took a deep breath. Gabriel fixed his eyes on her face and the slight flush in her cheeks. "Please," he said, as he held out the chair.

She sat, and he relaxed back against his desk, crossing his ankles in front of him. "The doctor assures me you are not mad and that you just need rest. For the time being, you will remain my guest. Lady Violet wishes to take you into town to shop for some clothing, as it appears that you do not have anything of your own."

Miss Bennett paled and smoothed a hand over her morning gown. She lifted troubled eyes to him. "Thank you for your generosity, Rothden. I don't want to be a burden or anything. I could help with dishes or cleaning or something while I'm here. But I… I have to get back home."

His chest tightened. "Do you have family waiting for you there? A husband and children?"

"No. No husband or children. Not even a boyfriend. I guess I'm what you would call a 'spinster'." She twined her fingers in her lap and looked down at them. "Just haven't met the right one, I guess. Or one who wants me, and not my sister." She shook her head and pushed at the corner of her spectacles. It seemed to be a nervous habit.

"You have a sister?"

"Yes. Bellamy is a fashion model. Uh, a woman who shows off the latest fashion in clothing."

He nodded.

"She's becoming very famous. She's so beautiful. You'd love her. She could have any man she wanted."

There was a mix of wistfulness and envy in her words, and he wondered at the cause. Was she jealous of her sister's beauty?

"I also have an older brother, Archer. He…he was injured in the military." Lily stood and paced away. "I found this little cabin in Corbin—that's in Kentucky, America—and I put in an offer on it. You know, because everyone needs a place to call home. A place to go to, even if you're jet-setting all over the world or you just want a home-cooked meal and time with your family…" Her voice trailed off as she neared the window.

Gabriel studied her silhouette. Her fingers were still clenched, and she held herself stiff. Talking about her family troubled her, he realized.

"You care for them."

She nodded. "We…we haven't been a family for several years. With Bellamy always traveling and Archer off on secret missions, we don't see each other or talk that much. I did the best I could when our parents died, but I could have done better. I *should* have done better. Maybe then Archer would return my calls."

The last words were spoken so softly, that Gabriel wondered if she realized that she'd said them aloud.

"One can only do their best," he said. "That must be enough."

"I wish that were true." Lily spun away from the window and pasted a smile on her face. "Sorry, I didn't mean to say all of that. Forget I said anything."

Gabriel fought the urge to reach for her again. It was as if her mask had slipped, and he'd gotten a brief glimpse of vulnerability beneath. A deeper, more personal vulnerability than she'd shown thus far, and it touched every protective instinct he had. He wouldn't let her retreat so quickly. "I know how difficult it can be to take on responsibilities after a parent's death," he said.

A look of surprise crossed her face. "You do?"

"Yes. I was still at Eton when my father died. I inherited the title earlier than expected and had to leave school to return here. I found the estate near financial ruin and my mother..." Gabriel gritted his teeth. "Not up to the task of providing Lady Violet with a proper upbringing. It was up to me to restore our finances and care for my sister."

Miss Bennett stepped closer, searching his face. "Like I did with Bellamy."

"You had to care for her? What of your brother?"

"He was already in the military and out of the country when they died. There was no one else. It was up to me."

A silent understanding passed between them.

Then she asked, "Everyone calls you Lord Rothden and she's Lady Violet. What title do you hold?"

A bemused grin touched his mouth. It had been so long since someone didn't know who he was that it felt odd to speak of it. "I am the Earl of Rothden."

Her eyebrows rose over the rim of her spectacles, and her pretty lips opened. "Oh, it's a title." She blushed. "I feel silly because I thought that was your first name. Like I'm Lily and you're Rothden."

Gabriel's lips twitched. "My given name is Gabriel Jacob Alexander Hawthorne, the Earl of Rothden and Baron Hawthorne."

"That's a mouthful. How do I address you? I mean, you can call me Lily, but what do I call you? Your Grace? No wait, that's a... duke?"

He chuckled. "Most people of my acquaintance call me Lord Rothden or Rothden."

Miss Bennett—Lily—nodded.

Only the closest of friends and family called him Gabriel. Society's rules of etiquette said that anything else simply wasn't done. He gave an internal snort. Society could go hang. This was his house, and he found that he did not want Lily to feel any more out of place than she already was. "You may call me Gabriel," he murmured.

She smiled then, and it lit up her face. The mousey woman behind the glasses went from lovely to stunning. He could scarcely breathe from the change.

"Gabriel," she said.

A rush of tingles shot through him at his name on her lips. *Rothden, get ahold of yourself.* She was a woman with no place to go, nothing to her name, and who may or may not be from some far future century. Which brought another thought to mind.

"Lily, you may have heard that I am hosting a house party. My guests begin to arrive tomorrow."

"Oh, I won't get in the way. I wouldn't fit in, and I don't want to embarrass you. I can keep to my room except for when I'm helping with the cleaning."

"You'll not be helping with the cleaning, Lily. I have plenty of hired servants to do that. As for not fitting in, Violet has agreed to help acclimate you to…Society." He couldn't say "their time". Gabriel still couldn't quite believe her story.

Lily must have sensed his hesitation. She nodded slowly. "You don't believe me. I guess, if the roles were reversed, I wouldn't believe me either."

"Lily…"

"No, I understand. Really. But I must find a way home. I don't belong here." She put her hand on his arm. "Thank you, Gabriel, for allowing me to stay."

He set his hand over hers as he often did with Violet. Her skin was soft. He feathered his thumb over the back of her palm. "Miss Bennett, I do not know that I can help you get home. But I will help however I can."

Lily smiled that sweet smile again and something shifted in his chest. He had to help her get back home. Something about this woman unsettled him in an uncomfortable way.

CHAPTER FIVE

V IOLET'S FIRST PRIORITY in acclimating Lily was to go shopping, which suited Lily just fine. She needed to return to the place where she'd first arrived and look for the clock. As they sat in the carriage on the way to the little village, she tugged at the bodice of her light green, muslin walking gown. It had very subtle stripes, another of the lacy scarves which she learned was called a *fichu*, and a cream bow in front. The dress was so feminine. For the first time in longer than she could remember, she felt pretty.

"One thing I like about this time is how nice everyone always looks," she said. "Dressing up to go out instead of just putting your hair into a messy bun and wearing your pajamas to get groceries."

Violet's brow scrunched. She sat on the cushioned seat opposite Lily. "I don't understand most of what you said."

Lily waved a hand. "I just meant that I like your dresses. Thank you again for loaning them to me."

The young woman's smile brightened. "We will have so much fun at the modiste. It's not the shops in London, but we'll find you a suitable wardrobe until we can get there. The fashion plates I've seen are beautiful. I can't wait to take you to the modistes on Bond Street in a couple of weeks. You've never seen such colors of silk."

Lily smoothed a hand over the muslin skirt. "You're going to London soon?"

"Of course, silly goose. The Season will begin not long after the Houses begin sessions. Gabriel normally uses a proxy for his seat in the House of Lords, but he still travels to London every year for the opening."

"When is that?"

"I believe we will depart not long after the house party is over. After All Saints."

Lily knew that was the beginning of November. Less than two weeks away. What if she didn't find the clock by then? She couldn't go to London. She was drawn to this particular place in this time. Wouldn't she have to be here to return home? Her chest tightened. *Don't panic, Lily. It's probably right there in the alley where you dropped it.*

She pulled the maroon velvet curtain aside and peered out the window. Most of the leaves had fallen from the trees and what remained were dark red, yellow, and brown. White curls of smoke rose from chimneys in the little hamlet, with houses clustered together. A church spire rose above them.

"Can we stop by the spot first?" she asked Violet. "If I find the clock, there may be no need to buy a wardrobe."

Violet tilted her head down and tucked her hands into her fur muff. "I suppose."

Lily realized that she'd disappointed her. She didn't know what to say. She had to get back home to try to mend her relationships with Bellamy and Archer.

The carriage rocked as it came to a stop. A footman in navy blue livery opened the door and held his hand out. Violet took it, lifted her skirt, and climbed down. Lily followed. The coach dipped as she stepped out, sending her head spinning. She pressed a hand to her temple until the world righted itself.

"Are you well?" Violet asked.

"Yes. I hope the dizziness goes away soon."

"Come on. The spot where we almost ran you down is over here. I think I shall call it 'Lily's Corner' to memorialize that spot." She tucked her arm through Lily's and walked down the sidewalk.

"I'm not certain it calls for fanfare," Lily said with a laugh.

"Of course, it does. How often does a woman from another time run in front of one's carriage? Now hurry so we can take a look at what gowns the modiste has."

They stopped in front of a vaguely familiar alley. Lily had been very jumbled up when she first opened her eyes. All she really remembered was the awful smell of rotting garbage and a brick wall. She'd never have found the alley if it weren't for Violet. The stench of rotting garbage filled her nose, and she covered her mouth to keep her breaths shallow.

The alley ran between two shops. To her left, gentlemen's top hats and beaver hats were on display at the milliner's next to frilly bonnets and satin turbans with peacock feathers. To her right, a man in a thick, brown coat used a handkerchief to mop his brow, then tucked it into his pocket and resumed sweeping the sidewalk in front of a brick store advertising shoes and repair. A pretty pair of ladies' boots and large, black riding boots were on display.

Lily scanned the sidewalk around her and the edge of the street where she'd stumbled in front of the carriage. Foul smelling liquids carried scraps of paper and other things that she didn't want to think about towards a drain. The holes were too small for her clock to fit through, so she turned her attention to the alley. She found a short piece of pipe and used it to search through all the refuse close to where she fell. *Damn.* The clock wasn't here.

She closed her eyes and tried to remember the moment she'd awakened. It had been raining, and she'd fallen on her hands and knees. She scanned the area once more.

"Anything?" Violet asked.

"No."

"Can I help the ladies?" the man said as he swept debris into the traveling channel of foul liquid. "Be you looking for sumpin?"

Lily straightened. "Yes. I was here the other day, and I think I dropped something. Have you seen a small, red enamel egg with gold trim?" She held up her hand to show him the approximate size.

He mopped his brow with his handkerchief again. "Aye, you be the woman what took a tumble in the road, eh?"

"Uh, yes."

"Good thing the lady here stopped, or you'd be with cocked up toes."

"You'd be dead." Violet whispered the translation at Lily's confused expression.

"Very good thing," she agreed. "Did you find anything like that or hear of an egg being found?"

"Nay, nuttin' of the like. And word'd be travelin' were sumpin' found of it. Of that, you be sure." He swept a few times over the sidewalk. "Sorry," he added after a moment. "Be I hearin' about it, I be sendin' word to you in that there fancy house, yeah?"

"Please," Violet said. Her attention snagged across the street. "Lily, if you're finished here, I think I spotted someone I know."

She took one last look around and then gave a resigned sigh. The clock wasn't here. "Is there anything special about this alley?" she asked the man.

He blinked at her a couple times, then bent and turned his head to look down the alley. "No? 'Tis cleaner than most, I'll grant you. Nothing be special though. Save you were in it." He winked.

That's cleaner than most? She shook her head and thanked the man.

Violet grabbed her arm and practically dragged her the opposite direction toward the dress shop. They passed right by the store and stopped beside a black carriage that was parked in front of the jeweler. She took one look at the carriage and then barged into the jewelry shop.

"Lord Musgrave!"

A handsome man of about thirty turned their way. He had brown hair and eyes with a square jaw. Lily didn't find him as attractive as Gabriel, but he had a lean waist, if not the widest of shoulders. He wore a brown cutaway coat over a red vest and tan pants. In one hand he held his top hat and a silver buckle in the other. He brightened as soon as he spotted Violet.

"My dear Lady Violet, you are as beautiful as the flower you are named after. Tell me, do you smell as sweet?"

"I wouldn't know." She gave him her hand, and he bent low over it to offer her a kiss.

One that lingered a bit, Lily thought. Hmm, did Violet have her eye on this gentleman? He definitely had his eye on her. His gaze swept over her pretty pink gown and back.

"Perhaps I shall have your brother distracted and find out for myself one day." He winked at Violet and then looked at Lily. "Forgive my manners, I am Musgrave. You must be a friend of Violet's."

"Yes. I'm Lily Bennett."

He held out his hand expectantly.

Oh, right. She placed her gloved fingers against his palm, and he bent low. His lips didn't brush the back, and she was oddly pleased about that.

"Miss Bennett is visiting from America and will be staying with us for the house party."

"I thought I detected an American accent. How delightful."

He didn't sound at all delighted. He looked back at Violet. "I believe your brother is hosting a country ball in a few days?"

She nodded. "And a masquerade. It will be ever so fun. Do you think I'll be able to find you in your costume?"

His gaze dropped to Violet's lips. "My dear, you may count on it. Would you save me a dance?"

Lily pretended to be interested in a glass case with men's rings.

"I should like that," her friend said a bit breathlessly.

"Then it is done. I shall see you at dinner tonight?"

"Yes. We are dress shopping for Miss Bennett first."

"I'll not keep you. Until tonight, Lady Violet."

Lily waved as they turned away and left the store.

"Isn't he handsome, Lily?" Violet pressed her hands to her red cheeks. "And he asked me for a dance. If Gabriel causes any trouble, will you please distract him for me? Just for one dance?"

"Why would he cause trouble?"

Violet rolled her eyes. "He's trying to turn me into a spinster. I'm so close to being on the shelf that the maid is about to dust me. It's like he doesn't want me to be happy. I'm of marriageable age. Half of my friends are already married, and Gabriel won't let a man near me without snarling like a wolf."

Lily chuckled at the mental picture. "He's probably trying to protect you."

"He can look away for one dance." They'd arrived at the dressmaker's shop. Violet threw the door open and marched in. "It's my house party, too, and I intend to have as much fun as possible. I may even steal a kiss with Lord Musgrave. Ha! That will show Gabriel."

"Uh, Violet, I don't think that's a good idea. I don't know your brother that well, but I don't think he'd be very happy."

She gave an unconcerned shrug. "Now, let's find you a new wardrobe."

Lily couldn't find the clock, which meant that she would be here for at least a few more days. She couldn't continue to borrow Violet's gowns. "Are you sure it's okay? We don't have to get much. I don't want you to have to spend a lot of money."

Violet laughed. "My brother said we should buy you a full wardrobe. He won't mind the expense. Besides, he worked very hard to get the estate financially stable. I think he takes pride in being able to care for those under his protection. We shouldn't take that pleasure away from him. Especially when it involves new dresses."

How could she argue with that? They spent the next several hours buying silk stockings, chemises, stays, and a half dozen different gowns. The modiste's assistant measured her, murmuring over her curves, and making chalk marks on where to let out the bust or take up the hem. Violet insisted on ordering a special costume for the masked ball, as well as a matching face mask.

The sun had begun to set by the time they left the shop with a dozen parcels. Lily sighed as she climbed into the carriage. They'd only been able to bring one gown with them. The others would be altered. But a small part of her was excited for the new clothes. She'd felt a bit like a princess today.

Don't get too comfortable, Lily. You still have to find a way home.

But what could she do without the clock? She might have dropped it in her apartment when she fell and hit her head. If the clock wasn't here, was she stuck here for good?

"SOMERSBY, IF YOU don't stop talking about the differences between a blunderbuss and a shotgun, I'm going to lock you in the cabinet with your precious weapons." Felton Seabright, the Viscount Seabright, emphasized each word by pointing his cigar at Somersby.

Gabriel should like to see that. In fact, if he didn't need Somersby to be his proxy in the House of Lords, he might have forgone an invitation to the man. As much as he appreciated a good weapon, there was only so much one could talk about them before becoming utterly bored. Somersby's tolerance for such talk exceeded everyone else's by a factor of five.

Edmund Somersby sat up straighter in his chair and flicked a lock of red hair off of his freckled brow. "It's little wonder that you're so terrible with your own weapon, Seabright. Perhaps you ought to take a child's gun to hunt Saturday so that no one is accidentally injured."

"If I don't, would you volunteer to be the injured party?" Seabright grinned and flicked ash from his cigar into the crystal dish.

Gabriel tuned out their good-natured bickering. And it was good-natured. The men were the best of friends and took delight in trading insults. He sipped his brandy and leaned back with his own cigar. Most of his friends had arrived today for the house party, with the remainder coming in tomorrow. After a filling dinner, the men remained behind to smoke and drink port, although Gabriel hated the stuff.

Violet and Patience Cradock, wife of Noah Cradock, had retired to the drawing room. Lily hadn't come down for dinner, and he found himself a bit disappointed. *It's the mystery she presents. Nothing more.*

If that wasn't entirely true, he chose not to examine it any further. No, he was exactly where he wanted to be. Surrounded by his friends, enjoying the last few days of freedom before the endless balls, dinners, plays, and salons where debutantes were lined up like lambs for the picking. And if they weren't picked, they were thrown at men like himself hoping one would catch him in marriage. Even having a mistress didn't dissuade most mamas who were determined to make a good match for their daughters. He shuddered.

"Do you think he sleeps with a gun?" Christian whispered from his right. There was a black smudge on the cuff of his sleeve, and his cravat looked as if it had been tied by a blind man. His blond hair was at least an inch longer than current convention, and he had a few days' beard growth.

Gabriel's lips twitched. "Quite likely," he murmured. They shared a quiet chuckle.

Christian Albury, the Earl of Huntington, was as close as a brother. They'd met at Eton, like the rest of this group of reprobates, and had formed a near unbreakable bond. There was nothing Gabriel wouldn't do for the man, and Christian had proved on more than one occasion that he felt the same.

"Thank you for coming to the house party," Gabriel said.

"Would you have let me do otherwise?"

"No."

"I thought as much. Hence why I'm here. Although I cannot see the appeal of it."

"That's precisely why I insisted that you attend." If it were up to his friend, he'd lock himself away in his workshop and not come out until the war with France was over. If then.

Most people looked upon Christian as a man lacking social skills with a tendency for abrupt, honest language when he did speak. He hated crowds, any sort of social engagement, and particularly anything to do with dancing. All of the things the Bon Ton loved. They didn't know that the Earl of Huntington possessed one of the most brilliant minds of their time. Indeed, he might one day rival the best renaissance men.

"I bet ten guineas that Somersby bags less grouse than Seabright," Owen Granville said. Of the seven men in attendance tonight, he was always the first to call for bets.

"Twenty," George Twisden added. "Twenty and a bottle of Rothden's best port." He raised his glass of brownish-purple wine and took a deep drink.

"You can't bet my port, Twisden," Gabriel said.

"What can I bet of yours?" he asked.

Hugh Musgrave let out a harsh laugh. "How about a dance with his sister?"

"Done!" Twisden bellowed. "Twenty guineas and a dance with Lady Violet. Who's taking?"

"No," Gabriel growled.

"I am," Musgrave said over Gabriel's sharp denial. "I bet the twenty guineas that Somersby bests Seabright by at least two birds."

"Speaking of birds, who was that lovely creature I spotted with your sister, Rothden?" Granville asked.

Gabriel cleared his throat. Lily had taken a tray in her room tonight, claiming a headache and a bit of dizziness. He suspected she was also nervous about being in a larger gathering. If she truly was from the future, as she claimed, then a dinner party might seem daunting. Hopefully Violet would instruct her more tomorrow. They'd returned giggling like schoolgirls earlier, and he was glad to see his sister happy.

"Rothden?" Granville called.

"That is Miss Lily Bennett from America. One of my sister's friends. She'll be staying for a time."

"Why did she not join us for dinner?" Instead of waiting for an answer, Granville turned to Seabright, Twisden, and Musgrave. "Miss Bennett is quite ah, well-formed." He made a rounding shape with his hands in front of his chest. "Very buxom. The green gown she wore barely contained her bosom."

Twisden sat forward in his chair. "Was she fair or plain?"

"I saw her with Lady Violet in Marston earlier. She is not entirely plain," Musgrave said.

"She's a pretty little thing," Granville stated. "If you overlook those dreadful spectacles."

Somersby groaned. "Must be a bluestocking. I hate when someone only talks about one subject for hours on end."

Seabright speared him with a disbelieving look. "Is that so?"

"You can't see her glasses if you've bent her over a table and tossed her skirts up," Twisden said.

"Enough," Gabriel growled. "Miss Bennett is not open for discussion."

"Staking a claim, Rothden? What of Lady Montrose?" Granville asked.

He thunked his glass down on the table. "Lady Montrose and I have ended our association. As for Miss Bennett, no one is staking *anything*. She is under my protection, so stow your cocks."

Twisden grinned. "If you've put Caroline to the curb, I may have a go. A few days romp in that vixen's bed is just what I need."

"What you need is a knock to the head," Noah Cradock said. "Patience read the society paper to me just this morning about how you were caught with your pants around your ankles by Major Waler as you plowed his wife."

"Nonsense. I was halfway out the door with my trousers firmly buttoned."

Granville shook his head. *The Gazette* got it wrong. Trousers around his ankles was with Zinnea Parling."

Gabriel's friends laughed. All except Christian, who sighed and reached into his pocket. He pulled out a small metal ring with gears attached to it and started fiddling with it.

Gabriel envied the man his focus on his passions. He hadn't felt able to indulge himself in anything for years. This house party was supposed to change that. Although, the first night had arrived and already he felt restless.

"...she accused me of carousing at Boodle's. The audacity." Seabright ground his cigar out and reached for another in his waistcoat.

"Absurd. You only carouse at White's," Somersby replied.

"Exactly what I told the old bat," Seabright said. "As if it is any of her business how I attend myself. She may be my aunt, but she has no control over my inheritance. I do as I please. If I want to spend every guinea I own, I shall."

"You wouldn't be the first man to become destitute between the thighs of—"

Gabriel pinched the bridge of his nose as a headache set in. As young men at Eton, they'd formed a bond in their Dame's house, as much to ward off bullies as to help each other with their studies. Of course, as young men of a certain fortune, the older they grew, the more dissolute they became. But when his father died, he'd left much of that life behind.

As his friends told bolder and often more bawdy tales of past pursuits, Gabriel found his ire growing. Men of thirty-one acting like young bucks, gallivanting around town, drinking, and carousing. Granted they had far less obligations. Of the lot, only he and Christian had inherited their titles. Is that why he was feeling out of sorts? As if he could no longer relate to these men he'd called friends for nearly two decades?

Christian seemed to have tuned them out, as he now had a tool and two small gears laid on the table and was currently attaching a third to the metal structure in his hand.

Gabriel swirled the brandy in his glass. Perhaps after he had Violet settled with a husband, he would spend more time in London and enjoy more of its entertainments. Drinking and gaming at White's until all hours, or visiting a courtesan well-trained in her craft.

Blast. The thought had all the appeal of a turn in Newgate. What did it say about him that he'd rather prowl balls and dinner parties to find Violet a husband than spend time doing what many men of his station did?

And dammit, he wasn't ready to find Violet a husband.

Unbidden, Lily came to mind as she'd stood in his garden yesterday, with the pale light shining down on her slumped shoulders, looking lost. He found the mystery of her far more enticing than a night out in Town. What if what she said was true? What did the world look like in her time?

"What say you, Rothden?"

Gabriel looked up to find Granville, Twisden, and Musgrave looking at him expectantly. He swallowed the last of his brandy and set the crystal glass on the table. This was the first night of his house party. He needed to entertain his guests, not ponder wild stories. "I say it is time to join the ladies. Anyone for a game of whist?"

Chapter Six

T HANK GOD FOR Regency romance novels. Lily had read enough
that it made her earlier crash course in the topic at least a little
easier. If she ever read another, she would definitely appreciate their
research.

Violet spent most of the day teaching Lily proper ways to address
the upper and lower classes. What to talk about and how to avoid
scandal. She learned how to take tea and pour for guests. Even what
conversation to make at dinner. Her brain felt stuffed, and she had no
idea if she could keep it all straight.

By the end of the afternoon, Lily felt the blossom of a friendship
with Violet. They'd laughed together, and she felt the same warmth
she used to feel during the good times with Bellamy. The feelings were
bittersweet.

*If I get home, I'm not going to give up until Bellamy and I have that kind
of friendship.*

Violet knocked twice on the door and then stepped into the bedroom. She never waited for Lily to invite her to enter, she simply
breezed into the room with a smile. She wore a burgundy dress with
bright gold and black embroidery in a thick band at the hemline. The
deep color brought out her fair skin and brown curls.

"Lily, how lovely you are! I knew that gown would become you."

She smiled and smoothed a hand over the satin. "Thank you. I've never worn anything so beautiful."

"You should wear silks and satins and velvets every day," Violet declared as she walked to where Lily stood at the window, overlooking the driveway. Another black carriage had arrived moments ago, and a tall man with white-blond hair stepped out. He wore a dark suit jacket that fit his wide shoulders to perfection, and tan pants.

"Zeph is here!" her friend said with enthusiasm.

"Who is he?"

"Lord Zeph Lael. He's one of my brother's dear friends. They've known one another for years. Most of the people arriving are his friends from boarding school. I'll introduce you tonight at dinner."

"Dinner? No, I thought I would stay—"

Violet shook her head and grabbed Lily's hand. "I didn't loan you that dress so you could stay in your room tonight. You did very well today. Tonight will be your chance to practice."

Lily groaned. Visions of pouring tea in someone's lap and shocking a room into silence with some faux pas filled her head.

"I'm going to mess up and say the wrong thing. I don't want to embarrass you and Gabriel."

"That is why this is the perfect scenario. It is a far more relaxed setting than a drawing room in Town. Wouldn't you rather practice here before facing the gossips in London? Unless you decide to dance naked on the dinner table, you needn't worry about doing the wrong thing." She tapped her lip with one finger. "Actually, if you did dance naked on the table, I daresay you would be quite popular. These *are* Gabriel's friends. They're often in the society paper for their scandals."

"Is Gabriel in the paper for scandals?" Lily flinched internally. *Shut up, Lily!* She hadn't meant to ask Violet about her brother, but curiosity got the better of her. Gabriel's tenderness during their conversation yesterday had drawn her attention more than his dark good looks already had. She'd spent half of last night wondering about him.

"Heavens, no. My brother is too buttoned up for that. He might take the occasional mistress, but he's not the sort to carouse like many of his friends. When Father died and the earldom passed to him, he threw himself into bettering the estate. I think he's forgotten how to enjoy himself."

Lily imagined Gabriel laughing. He'd have a dark, husky chuckle. The kind that made a woman wet just hearing it. She suppressed a shiver at the thought.

"Don't fret, Lily. You'll do well, and you look beautiful."

Lily looked down at the dinner gown. It was a beautiful peacock-blue satin with puffy cap sleeves and an emerald green ribbon, embroidered with seed pearls, at the bottom of the empire waist. The ribbon tied in a simple bow in back, and the long tails trailed down to the top of the mini train. The hem was embroidered with shimmery crystals that were muted until caught by the candlelight. Once again, the bodice was quite snug, and the low, square neckline pushed the tops of her breasts up, drawing the eye.

Lily almost laughed. She'd never worn something so revealing while wearing this many layers. Actually, she rarely wore anything revealing. Jeans and tee shirts were more her style.

She wasn't falling for a hot guy again. Especially not an earl who lived two centuries in her past. It didn't matter what Gabriel thought when he saw her tonight, and she wasn't thinking about it. At all. Or wondering what he would think of the other gowns they'd purchased, like the gold one. And the emerald green.

"Don't you like the dress?" Violet asked as the silence stretched. "I could bring you another, although we'll be late for dinner."

"What? No. I'm just nervous. Thank you for everything."

"I'm happy you're here, Lily. It's been deadly dull these last months." Violet squeezed her hand. "Come on. I can't wait for Gabriel to see you," she said as she pulled Lily toward the door.

They descended the stairs to the hall. Gabriel stood with the newly arrived Lord Lael and another man with blond hair.

"Zeph!" Violet raced down the last few steps and flung herself into the taller man's arms. The impact set him back a step, but Violet didn't seem to notice. "I didn't know you'd be here."

He winked and flicked her nose with his finger. "And miss seeing my favorite flower?"

She laughed and turned to throw her arms around the other man. "Christian, I didn't get a hug yesterday."

Christian patted her back rather awkwardly, as if he didn't know what to do with his hands. "Hello, Violet."

Lily grinned at the young woman's exuberance. Then she realized that Gabriel was watching her. She almost missed the last step. *Get it together, Lily.* She swallowed and gave him a shaky smile.

Gabriel wore a dark navy-blue coat that emphasized the width of his shoulders and beneath which was a gold waistcoat. His white cravat and high collars made his bronze skin and masculine jawline stand out. It was a moment before she could force her gaze up to meet his.

Their eyes locked for only a moment, then he slowly took in her gown. "You look quite lovely, Miss Bennett," he said at last.

The low rumble of his words, spoken quietly, sent a small thrill through her.

"You're very handsome, Gabr... Lord Rothden." She cast a quick glance at the second man, relieved that he didn't seem to notice her slip up.

Gabriel's lips twitched. "You may call me Gabriel. You'll find my friends unconcerned with the propriety of titles." He turned to the men at his side. "Christian, Zeph, may I present Miss Bennett. She's an acquaintance of my sister's and has come to stay for a time. Miss Bennett, this is Lord Christian Albury, the Earl of Huntington." He waved to the darker blond man with stormy blue-grey eyes. A few days' whisker growth shadowed his jaw and his cravat looked crooked.

"And Lord Zeph Lael." He gestured to the man with that unusual white-blond hair. His eyes were also unique, almost silver. She'd never seen another with his coloring.

Lily tried a short curtsey and managed to make it look somewhat graceful. She did a mental fist pump.

"Miss Bennett." The earl, Christian, took her hand and bowed over it. A slight pink tinged his cheeks, and he stepped back quickly. The faint scent of oil clung to him. "Please, call me Christian. I don't wish to be reminded of my title."

"Okay. Call me Lily."

He gave a slight bow.

Zeph elbowed him out of the way to take her hand and repeat the greeting. Only he brushed his kiss over the back of her hand and a zing of electricity shot up her arm. She sucked in a breath, and he winked.

"Behave, Lael," Gabriel said. He inserted himself between her and Zeph, and his friend grinned.

"She's American. Isn't that wonderful?" Violet said as she looped her arm through Christian's and fairly dragged the man towards the dining room.

Zeph followed. "Indeed. I'm often fascinated with how far people travel in this time."

Lily stared after him. Something about him seemed odd. She mentally snorted at herself. As if she could talk.

Gabriel held his arm out. "Shall we, Lily? I don't wish to keep my guests waiting."

Lily took his arm and let him lead her to the dining room. The warmth of his body washed over her. She leaned closer. God, he smelled good. Like pine and masculine musk. She wanted to press her face to his neck and breathe him in. Her belly warmed at the mental image, tempting her.

He dipped his head down. "The color of that gown is quite becoming on you, Lily. I fear my friends will be so entranced that I will lose them all to you."

His warm breath brushed the sensitive spot behind her ear as he spoke. Had she ever been so aware of a man? She felt her cheeks flush. "Thank you. But if they do, it will not be the color of the dress that's catching their eye." She waved her hand in front of her chest. "Violet's gowns enhance certain things. It will be nice to have a few dresses that fit better. Oh! Thank you for those. I told Violet that we didn't have to buy so much, but she insisted."

His soft laugh stole over her, making goose bumps break out on her arms and her nipples tighten. They paused just outside of the dining room, and Gabriel turned to face her. His gaze swept over her body once more, lingering briefly, before finding hers. "I'm certain you will look beautiful in them all."

She took a small step forward. "I'll try not to embarrass you in there tonight."

One side of his mouth tugged up. "I'm far more concerned about my friends embarrassing me."

Lily smiled.

Gabriel raised his fingers toward her cheek but dropped his hand before touching her. "Shall we, Lily?"

He escorted her into the dining room where his guests were already gathered. Lily was given the seat between Violet and Christian, while Gabriel took the seat at the head of the table on Violet's right. Besides the four of them, there were eleven other guests. Gabriel made introductions.

Lily studied the nine men and two women. They were all beautifully dressed, and there was an air of familiarity between them that said they'd known each other for years. A few sent curious glances her way, but Gabriel introduced her as Violet's friend and that seemed to quell their curiosity.

"Aunt Josephine couldn't be here," Violet said. "She claims the country air gives her a terrible cough, which apparently she doesn't get traveling to and from her friends' homes daily for gossip in the chilly London air."

Christian choked on his drink.

"We're all dreadfully disappointed," Gabriel said without an ounce of disappointment in his voice.

"Will she be my chaperone this Season?" Violet asked her brother.

He slanted her a look. "She will attend all parties with us, but you know as well as I that it is inherently difficult to chaperone a young lady while foxed and surrounded by your favorite gossips."

Violet rolled her eyes and mumbled something about "stuffy brothers".

Lily felt Christian shift beside her. He looked uncomfortable, though whether it was the setting or something else, she didn't know. Time to put her lessons to work.

"Lord Huntington, how long have you known Lord Rothden?"

Christian looked at her with raised eyebrows, and he rubbed his hands on his pant legs. "Christian, please."

She nodded.

"Gabriel and I have known one another since college at Eton. We met in our first year. He…insisted on being my friend."

When he looked over at Gabriel, she saw affection in his eyes, and something more. *Gratitude?* She cocked her head to the side and studied him.

Christian was taller than Gabriel by a few inches. His hair looked as if he'd run his fingers through it several times. Stormy, intelligent eyes met hers and then glanced quickly away. Sitting this close to him, the smell of oil was a bit stronger. When he reached for his wine glass, she noted a couple of dirt smudges on his hands.

"Gabriel seems the type to always get what he wants," she replied.

Christian gave a small smile. "Indeed. Hard to fight against a will so strong. It is one thing I admire greatly about him."

His tone said there was much more he admired. "What of you?"

she asked.

Christian's eyebrows rose. "I'm not nearly so strong of will."

She smiled. "Oh, I doubt that. But I meant for you to tell me about yourself. Violet seemed surprised to see you."

He shifted in his chair. "Gabriel insisted. He thinks I spend far too much time in my… at home."

Her heart softened. Christian was shy, she realized. This dinner party had to be his version of a nightmare. "I admire a man who would step out of his comfort zone for a friend," she said gently.

"Y-you do?"

"I do. I think it says a lot about a man's character. Where I come from, it seems like those sorts of friends are harder to find."

"Where is it you come from, Miss Bennett?"

"Lily," she reminded him. "I'm…from America."

He studied her for a moment. "How did you come to be friends with Violet?"

"We met recently."

"I almost ran her over with our carriage," Violet piped in.

"I shall try to remember to steer clear of you next time I see you in Hyde Park."

Violet laughed. "You may try." Then to Lily she said, "Christian is an inventor. He makes the most amazing things."

His cheeks flamed. "Please, Violet. No woman wants to hear about my dull habits."

So that's why he smelled of oil. "What sort of things do you invent?"

He shrugged.

"My…a man I knew I had this incredible desk that was built around…sometime recently. It was this mahogany behemoth with all the regular drawers. But it had hand cranks. One for each side. And when you turned the cranks, a row of drawers raised up in the back, or the top tilted for writing. It was fascinating. I'd never seen…"

Lily stopped talking when she realized that Christian sat complete-ly still, staring at her.

"What?"

Before he could reply, servers came forward with an array of food. Steaming soup, soft breads, fruit, and a roasted fowl. It smelled heavenly.

The man on Christian's left, George Twisden, engaged him in conversation and the odd moment passed.

"He's very sweet," Violet said. "I've never met a more shy man. Gabriel says he's the smartest man he's ever met, but I see him stammer over his words when speaking to a woman."

"Do you *like* him?"

"Of course, I… oh, you mean *like* him." Violet glanced at Christian, then shook her head. "Even if he wasn't my brother's dearest friend, I've known Christian so long that he seems like my brother." She made a face. "I couldn't kiss my brother."

Lily laughed. "I couldn't kiss mine either."

"Is he as overbearing as mine?"

Her smile faded. "No. Or at least, he didn't used to be. I don't know what he is anymore. He won't talk to me."

"Whyever not? Families should always talk to one another. Some-times, we're all each other has."

"I wish life was like that."

Violet waved a fork at her. "Life is exactly how you make it. If you want to be closer to your brother, then be closer to him." She paused. "Although in your case, that might be difficult."

Lily wished she had the enthusiasm for life that her friend did. Violet only saw adventure, not heartache or hardships. Had Gabriel truly sheltered her so much that she didn't see the bad, or did she simply not let it affect her? "When I get home, I'll try again. Archer was in the military, and he was badly injured. Since then, he hasn't returned any of my calls. Correspondence," she quickly corrected.

"Sometimes a man thinks he should be left alone," Christian said quietly. "Then someone like Gabriel comes along and drags them into Society, whether they wish to be or not. Only a fool thinks he is better off without someone like that in his life."

She hadn't realized he'd been listening.

He raiscd his glass to her, then turned back to Mr. Twisden, who was loudly telling a story about a game of cards.

Lily felt Gabriel watching her again. She met his gaze, then returned to her soup.

⁂

WAS THAT FATWIT Musgrave flirting with Violet? Gabriel squinted at the man standing a bit too close to Violet on the other side of the drawing room. They'd all adjourned here after dinner for tea, coffee, and desserts. He held a forgotten cup of tea, half-raised to his lips as he spotted the two conversing. Musgrave's dark head was bowed towards her as if hanging on her every word, and a smile played on his mouth. Violet smiled and waved her hands as she spoke, no doubt regaling the man with some adventure she'd attempted. His sister sparkled with life and enthusiasm in everything she did. Gabriel loved her for it, but she often drew unwanted attention.

He was contemplating how to nicely put his fist in his friend's face when the cushion of the sofa he sat on dipped.

Zeph sat beside him, stretched his long legs out, and crossed his ankles. "Do you suppose Musgrave realizes that his front teeth are in jeopardy?" he asked. A glint of humor sparkled in his eyes.

"Unlikely, or he would have taken his mouth away from my sister." He set his teacup on the small table in front of him.

Zeph chuckled. "He does appear smitten. She is beautiful, charming, intelligent, and the sister of an earl. It's a wonder men do not trail behind her." He slanted a look at Gabriel from the corner of his eye.

"Or perhaps it isn't."

"I'm only protecting her from the likes of men like him," Gabriel huffed and waved a hand toward Musgrave. "Violet has a soft and loving heart. I don't want it shattered by some fop only interested in a conquest."

"How will you know the difference when the time comes if none are allowed to approach her?"

"Simple. I'll pick one out myself."

Zeph laughed. "I do hope you'll let me watch when you have that conversation with your sister." He unfolded himself from the sofa and stood. "In the meantime, I think I will rescue Musgrave from an early grave." He started to leave, then turned back. "Careful, Gabriel. Suitors are not the only men who can break her heart."

Gabriel scowled at his friend's back. Zeph was wrong. He was Violet's guardian, and as such, it was his responsibility to insure she married a man of good standards and financial responsibility. She was an intelligent girl. She would understand the wisdom of him making the choice for her.

A light laugh from his right drew his attention to the spot he'd studiously avoided since they entered the drawing room. Lily sat at a small table across from Christian, with a backgammon board between them. She wore a light shawl over her lovely blue gown. Even though a fire crackled in the hearth, there was a nip in the air from the cold, drizzling rain outside. With her tortoiseshell glasses and shiny dark curls that appeared to be threaded with caramel, her pretty lips, and shy demeanor, Miss Lily Bennett was entrancing.

He was not the only one to notice. Throughout dinner, several of his friends shot curious and heated glances her way. Even Christian, who rarely spoke to women, smiled at her over the game. His cheeks were a ruddy pink as he let out a soft chuckle.

Gabriel's gut twisted. He wanted to march over there and take Christian's place. To keep her smiles and shy looks for himself. Good

Christ, he was going mad. Gabriel ran a hand over his face and then set his teacup on the table at his elbow. Christian *needed* this, he reminded himself. His best friend would rather turn in the other direction than speak to a beautiful woman.

Not because he didn't like them. Quite the contrary. Christian had often confessed to feeling awkward and unsure in a female's company. Afraid that anything he said would be too far above a young lady's intelligence or too dimwitted to keep their attention. Lily seemed to have no issue engaging the man. Twice, she'd made Christian smile at dinner. Gabriel should have been happy, not biting back his annoyance.

"You look as if you want to box someone's ears," Violet said.

Gabriel yanked his stare away from Lily and Christian and found his sister standing in front of him. She bent to kiss his cheek then sat beside him on the sofa.

"Christian seems to like her," she added as she looked over his shoulder at the couple playing backgammon.

"He's being polite."

Violet pressed her lips together and made a noncommittal noise. "I don't think I've ever seen him smile at a woman like that. Have you? The way he's leaning in close, shooting glances at her while she ponders her next move... I think they could make a lovely match. Wouldn't you agree, dear brother?"

He scowled at Christian. "I don't think he's the right man for..." he trailed off when he turned back to Violet and saw the wicked twinkle in her eyes. His jaw muscle twitched. "She's a beautiful woman, and any man would find her attractive." Gabriel ground the words out between clenched teeth.

"Even you?"

"What do you want, Violet?"

"I came to tell you that your services are required tomorrow."

"In what regard?"

"You must teach Lily how to dance."

He blinked. "What?"

Violet laid a hand on his arm. "Gabriel, the country dance is coming up, followed by the masked ball. Someone will ask her to dance, and she doesn't know any of the steps."

"Why can't you teach her?" He wanted to hold Lily in his arms again. Far more than was proper since he barely knew the woman.

His sister gave him a look that said he was a fatwit. "I don't know the gentleman's part."

He sighed. "Reginald could—"

"Are you really going to ask your steward to teach Lily to dance? If so, then I shall ask someone else. Perhaps Lord Musgrave or Lord Twisden would be more inclined to help. Yes, definitely Lord Twisden. I always see him dancing with ladies."

"Not Twisden," he growled. "And stay away from Musgrave."

Violet crossed her arms over her chest and glared at him. "How do you propose I stay away from a guest in my own house? Should I barricade myself in my room until they're gone? Is there a tower in this house you would prefer to lock me in?"

"Violet…"

"I won't have her become a wallflower because you don't want to concern yourself. Go on your hunt or whatever it is you have planned for tomorrow." She waved her hand airily. "Perhaps Lord Granville and Lord Wadham will stay behind."

Gabriel blew out a harsh breath and bared his teeth. All he wanted for this fortnight was to relax and enjoy a bit of sport and cards with his friends. Now he would have to forgo the hunt, because he'd be damned if he'd let one of these reprobates hold Lily close while teaching her to dance. Damn Violet for being right. Lily would feel out of place and would end up the subject of gossip if she didn't dance a single step.

"Fine. Tomorrow," he growled.

Violet clapped her hands and pressed a kiss to his cheek. "You'll have fun, I promise. You won't even miss the hunt."

Gabriel shook his head. He already did.

CHAPTER SEVEN

L ILY GASPED AND held her side, then laughed as she tried to catch her breath. Across from her, Christian ducked his head and a smile twitched the corners of his lips. She'd just tripped over his feet again. She'd given up counting how many times she'd trampled the poor man's toes.

After breakfast, most of the guests rode out on a hunt in the woods at the back of the estate. Only Gabriel, Violet, Christian, Lily, and Patience Cradock stayed behind. Violet led them into the salon where they spent the next several hours attempting to teach Lily to dance.

She giggled. Dancing in modern times was so different than the choreographed steps of these dances. Some people still ballroom danced. There was even a popular television show dedicated to it. But she'd never tried. Never had anyone even remotely interested in learning with her.

"No one dances where you're from, Lily?" Violet asked. She ushered Lily back into her starting spot for the gallopade.

"They do. But only a few dance like this. Mostly it is just moving bodies to music." Lily said when she could breathe normally. The gallopade was as fast as the polka she'd seen performed at a festival one time. Just a few turns around the room and she was out of breath. *Jeez, I need to exercise more.*

"Again," Gabriel said in that rich voice that sent shivers through her. He was so damn handsome in his dark green jacket and embroidered waistcoat. A lock of hair fell over his forehead, giving him a rakish look. He moved Christian aside to take his place across from Lily.

Violet grinned and pulled Christian into the spot in front of her.

Patience sat at the pianoforte near the windows, playing the music for each dance. She was a quiet young woman with pretty gray eyes. A little plumper than Violet, she had a kind smile. She played the opening notes to the gallopade.

Gabriel bowed to her, his eyes never leaving her face. Lily's heart thumped, and not from the exertion. He'd only danced once with her today. The first quadrille. She'd accidentally stepped on his foot when she'd turned the wrong direction. He'd grimaced, and when the set was over, he exchanged places with Christian to be Violet's partner. That put poor Christian in the line of fire for her clumsy footwork. But the shy man never once complained. He guided her in the right step as often as possible and laughed with her as she muddled her way through.

After three hours, Lily had successfully danced a quadrille and a minuet without maiming her dance partner. That seemed to be the test criteria. If she didn't step on anyone's foot through an entire piece of music, she was deemed a suitable enough dancer to move on to the next dance.

Thank God for their low standards. Any higher, and she might never learn another dance. She wasn't confident that she could dance the same thing twice without inflicting harm on some poor man's toes.

Lily looked at Gabriel and pressed her lips together. She wanted to dance with him. As fun as it was to partner with Christian, she wasn't drawn to him like she was Gabriel. Though none of the dances had couples holding each other very close, she wanted to feel Gabriel's heat against her side, breathe in his scent, and look up into his face.

He extended his hand to her. She curtsied and placed her palm in his.

Gabriel drew her a bit closer to put his hand on her waist, and they started the quick galloping steps in a circle around the room.

Please, please don't step on his foot, Lily!

Now that he was willing to dance with her again, she didn't want to screw up. He might give up on her entirely.

"Turn," he said softly just before she was to step in front of him so he could swing them to face the opposite direction.

She turned in time to the music and stepped back into the next galloping step.

"Excellent, Lily," he murmured. His eyes never left hers.

Being in his embrace was incredible. All her admonishments to stay away from the beautiful man were forgotten, and she lost herself in the dance. He spun her into one last turn, then bowed as the music slowed to a stop.

Lily curtsied, then wrapped an arm around her waist. She felt dizzy and breathless. *From the dance or him?*

"Perfect," Gabriel said. His thumb stroked over the back of her hand. He didn't release her.

"I-I'm sorry I stepped on you earlier," she stammered.

Something moved through his eyes. "Not at all, Lily. You're learning remarkably fast."

"Thank you for showing me the steps, even if I'm not here to use them. I haven't had this much fun in a long time." And she *was* having fun. Despite the embarrassment of constantly tripping over her feet and theirs, between the teasing and the laughter, she felt...embraced. Welcomed. Like she'd found a new set of friends who liked her the way she was. Even when she didn't know anything about dancing or etiquette.

She'd started the day feeling like a fish out of water. Like every move she made turned the opposite direction of where she was supposed to be.

Just like my life, she thought. *Always facing the wrong way.*

But now, with Gabriel looking down at her with one side of his mouth quirked and Violet's strong laugh to her left, Lily felt a small change. A connection with Gabriel, Violet, Christian, and even Patience. Like deepening friendship.

She squeezed Gabriel's hand and smiled up at him.

"You did it!" Violet cried as she jostled her brother aside and threw her arms around Lily. "I think you're getting better with each turn."

"We should do one more set," Gabriel said.

Violet shook her head. "We do not have time. The hunting party will be back shortly."

Lily's heart sank. "We're done?"

"No. There's one more dance to learn." Violet's eyes lit up. "The waltz."

Christian choked. Behind Gabriel, Lily saw Patience duck her head and pretend to study the pianoforte keys.

"Violet—" Gabriel said sharply.

She ignored him. "It's a scandalous dance," she said with excitement. "Many of the hostesses are beginning their balls with it, even though there are weekly letters to the newspaper decrying it as indecent."

"The waltz is indecent?" Since when? It was a formal dance, not the Argentinean tango where dancers practically wrapped their bodies around each other. Visions of wrapping her body around Gabriel danced through her mind, making her skin heat. She met his gaze.

He held it, and she wondered if he was thinking the same.

Of course, he isn't, Lily. But God, she just wanted him to.

The disbelief in her voice made Violet giggle. "It's true. But we'll have a waltz at the masquerade, won't we Gabriel?"

He looked at Lily another long second, then said, "Even if we do, you may not dance to it, Violet."

She crossed her arms over her chest. "Why not?"

"You're an unwed young lady."

"So? Lily's not married, are you?"

"Uh, no?" Lily looked between Violet and Gabriel. It was just a waltz though, right? Unless that was code for some dirty dancing Regency style. When brother and sister glared at one another, Lily looked past them to Christian. He seemed to find his boots very fascinating.

"Whether Miss Bennett is married or not has no bearing on you dancing the waltz. There will be many more people here that night. Word of you dancing a waltz could have disastrous consequences to your reputation. After all your begging for me to allow you a match, you would ruin that just to dance a waltz?"

"We're in the country, Gabriel. This isn't Almack's." Violet's voice rose with each word. Her arms were crossed tightly over her chest, and she leaned forward into Gabriel's space, practically shouting the words.

Uh oh. This looked very familiar. She'd been on the receiving end of many such stances when she and Bellamy argued, which was often. Almost daily, the last few years before Bells went to college and then started modeling. Even though Violet wasn't Bells, Lily had a sinking feeling she knew exactly how this argument would end. She and Gabriel were a little too much alike in this regard.

The only difference was, he hadn't lost his sister yet.

"It doesn't have to be Almack's or London for gossip to reach there," he growled. "Many of the guests will arrive there shortly after we do. You don't think they'll have whispered among each other? You're not waltzing."

"Yes, I am."

Lily stepped in between them. "It's okay. I don't need to learn the waltz. Maybe I should practice the minuet again. Otherwise, any potential dance partners may be maimed like poor Christian."

Violet continued to glare at her brother.

Gabriel sighed. "I will teach you the waltz, Lily. Violet, we will speak of this later. For now, sit."

Violet spun in a swirl of white skirts and flounced over to a chaise. She dropped into it with a mutinous expression.

"I'll...sit with her," Christian said.

Gabriel took Lily's arm and led her to the middle of the small dance space.

"Thank you," he murmured. "A few more moments and Violet and I would have had a loud row."

"It's really hard to be both sibling and parent. I imagine it's hard for Violet to be both sibling and child in your eyes."

"I'm only trying to do what is best for her."

"I know. But it's hard for her to see that right now. Bellamy was the same."

"How did you make your sister see reason?" he asked.

Lily looked down at her slippers. "I never did. By the time she left for college, we were barely on speaking terms. Hopefully when I get home, I can find a way to fix that."

Warm fingers brushed her jaw and tilted her head up. "You will."

She smiled.

Gabriel put his hand on her waist and drew her closer.

Her breath caught. The room around them faded until all she saw was him. All she smelled was the warm pine scent of his skin, and all she felt was the heat of his body. The air between them felt charged. Was he going to kiss her?

He lowered his head a fraction.

She waited, afraid to break the spell.

"Shall we waltz, Miss Bennett?" he whispered near her ear.

Pianoforte music began to play. Before disappointment could sink in, he took her hand in his, raised it up, and spun her in a circle around the room.

>>><<<

WHY WAS IT that when one needed sleep, it often proved elusive? Gabriel rolled onto his back and stared at the canopy above his head. His thoughts tumbled upon themselves, Miss Lily Bennett at the center of them all. Her laugh as she stepped on toes during the quadrille or her delighted smile when she mastered a step. She'd had Christian chuckling, which was a minor miracle in itself.

The way she fit against him as he taught her the waltz…

How her eyes shone as she stared up at him. With joy, but with something deeper. Interest, attraction. She'd been entrancing.

Gabriel shifted to his stomach and covered his head with the pillow. His night shirt tangled in his legs and he fought to free himself. With a curse, he sat up and yanked the velvet bed curtain aside. If he couldn't keep his mind off of the woman on his own, he'd go to the library and find the dullest book on the shelves to read until sheer boredom put him to sleep.

He yawned as he pulled on his dressing gown and tied the belt as he left his chamber. He paused next to Lily's door, listening for the slightest sound of her slumber. It shamed him that he couldn't walk by the lady's chamber without hoping for some small sound of her presence. When he heard nothing, he grit his teeth and made himself descend to the library.

What kind of man hovered outside a woman's chamber door in the dark of night, listening for her movements? Not one Lily would want to associate herself with. Gabriel muttered a curse at himself and stomped down the last few steps.

The library door was partially open and faint light spilled out. There was no moon tonight, so the room should have been dark. He put his hand on the heavy wood door and pushed it open to peer inside.

There, Lily held a candle as she searched the bookshelves. Waves of dark hair cascaded down between her shoulders. She wore only a thin night rail. Not even a wrapper for modesty. The shadows danced around her curvy body as she moved and hinted at what lay beneath. His cock took notice and began to rise.

Gabriel slipped in silently and moved closer. The golden candle-light lit up her pale, creamy skin, and the way she tugged her bottom lip between her teeth as she bent to study the book titles. The thin night dress molded over her bottom as she bent. *Thank God the library was shadowed in darkness,* he thought as he adjusted his cock.

"Having trouble sleeping?" he asked.

Lily jumped and candle wax splattered onto her hand. "Ow. Damn." She set the candle on the closest table, next to a stack of books, and rubbed the wax off of her skin.

Gabriel captured her hand in his and held it toward the light.

"It's okay," she said. "It didn't burn badly. You just surprised me."

"I should have been more careful." He lifted her hand to his lips and placed a kiss over the slight red mark on her skin.

Lily shivered, and her lips parted.

Her hand was soft in his and he could smell her rose bath soap. He released her and turned to the haphazard pile of books. "What are you looking for?"

"I thought maybe I could find the maker of the little clock." She shrugged. "Doubtful, but I have to try something. I don't know what else to do."

"You're concerned for your siblings."

She nodded. "I know that they're old enough to take care of themselves. It's just...I sort of...feel like a failure for not being close with them. You're supposed to be close with your family. I spent so long trying to keep our old house and make sure that we had enough to eat, that I didn't have enough left to spend time with Bellamy doing the things we used to enjoy. Sometimes I worked two jobs, so when she came home from school at night, I wasn't there."

Gabriel saw something of himself in her. She worked hard to improve her family's financial circumstances while struggling to raise a younger sibling. He understood her feelings perfectly. "Yet you succeeded? You did not go hungry or lose your house?"

"No, we didn't. But the effort put too much strain on our relationship. I suppose we were both still hurting from the deaths of our parents, and that made things even worse. God, the arguments we had." She shook her head. "At least I helped her get into a good college. For a little while. She dropped out to model. I was so mad. I never had the chance to go to college, and it felt like she was throwing away the opportunity just to spite me."

"Was she? Trying to spite you?"

"She said she wanted to travel. I guess I can't blame her for that. That's why Archer joined the military. Between the two of them, they've been all over the world."

He heard the wistfulness in her voice. It seemed Lily sacrificed more than her time and her opportunity for college in raising her sibling. He suspected she'd sacrificed her dreams as well. "Now that you are no longer obliged to care for a younger sibling, did you have plans to travel?"

"I moved around a little after I sold our old house. Trying to find a place that felt like home. But I never made it overseas." She huffed a laugh. "Until now, apparently."

A smile tugged at his lips. "You envy them."

Her eyes flicked to his in surprise. "No, I…well, yes, I guess I do. A little. I'm glad that they have seen and done the things they wanted to."

"But you have not."

She ducked her head. "Not yet."

"If you return to your time, what plans did you have to do those things? To travel and further your education?"

"Uh, none. I'm trying to buy a little cabin. That way when Bellamy and Archer come to visit, they have a place to stay. After I do that, maybe I'll think about traveling."

"What about a family of your own? A husband and children?" His stomach tightened unaccountably at the thought.

"Some future dream, I suppose."

"Any other future dreams?"

Lily chewed her lip. "There should be."

"Perhaps it is time to think about the things that you want, Lily."

"Maybe. Right now, I want to find a clock maker. All I found was a book on the theory of trade in the world."

"Excellent choice. That book should put you right to sleep."

"Would you like one for yourself?" Lily handed him the book. Her eyes crinkled at the corners when she smiled.

"Ah, no. I was hoping for something even more dull. *The General View of Agriculture* perhaps."

"At home, I read every night in bed. It helped settle my mind so that I could sleep."

"What did you read?"

"Romance. I only read romances."

His Lily was a romantic. Did she read them and dream of a great romance of her own?

"I don't suppose you have any?" she asked, although by her tone, she thought he wouldn't.

His lips tugged up. "Violet snuck a few romances into the library, hoping that I wouldn't notice." He reached behind her, pressing himself that much closer, to run a finger over the leather spines.

She sucked in a breath.

The air changed between them, like the charge before a lightning strike. Heady and breathless. Something about this woman drew him. The more he learned about her, the more he desired her. Her strength and intelligence shone through every conversation, and Gabriel found himself deeply attracted to that combination.

Gabriel rested his other hand on the bookshelf, caging her in. He looked down into her eyes, illuminated only by the candle flame. The darkness wrapped around them, cocooning them in shadows. A branch brushed the window outside, and the house creaked. The silence of the night cast a spell, weaving between them, tugging them closer. It was as if they'd slipped into the land of dreams, where nothing felt real.

Lily pressed her hands to his chest. She didn't push him away.

He wanted to feel her soft hands against his bare skin, but his dressing gown and sleep shirt were in the way. She stroked over his chest, then dipped her fingers under the edge of his velvet robe.

Closer to where he wanted her hands.

He dipped his head and traced his nose along her hairline, breathing her in. She arched into him, brushing her hips against his.

Her eyes widened when she felt his hard cock, and a shuddering breath left her lips.

"You fit against me perfectly," he whispered. "When we danced, this is what I imagined."

Her hands quested up to the open neckline of his sleep shirt and pushed it aside. She followed with her mouth, the lightest brush of satin lips over the base of his throat.

Gabriel sucked in a sharp breath, and his hips bucked against hers of their own accord. He cupped her cheek and tilted her face up to his. Sleepy eyes met his, and he realized that she wasn't wearing her glasses. He pressed a kiss over one eyelid and then the other.

She slid one hand up his chest to cup the back of his head.

He feathered a kiss at the edge of her lips, a light touch meant only to tease. She trembled in his embrace. Gabriel moved lower, brushing his mouth just barely over her jaw and down the column of her throat. Her scent drove him mad. Wound around him until all he could smell was Lily.

The neck of her night rail was open, leaving a tempting vee for him to follow. He lost himself to the temptation and traced her skin with his mouth.

Her fingers speared into his hair, gripping the strands and holding him closer. Ah, his Lily was passionate. He wanted to lay her out on the library table and feast from her mouth, her skin, the heat between her legs.

She yanked his head back up and pressed her mouth to his.

Gabriel growled with need. His hands smoothed down her back to cup her arse and hold her tighter against his erection.

Lily bit his bottom lip.

The slight sting made his lips part, and she took advantage, sliding her tongue against his.

Good Christ. Gabriel felt half mad with want. He fisted the skirt of her night dress and yanked it up until his hand met warm skin. He traced her satiny thigh up to her hip and to the round, soft fullness of her buttocks.

Lily moaned against his mouth and kissed him harder.

He turned her toward the table, shoved the books aside, and hoisted her up onto it. The damn night rail was in the way. He pushed the hem up to her hips, spread her knees, and pulled her closer to the edge of the table.

Her hands dropped to the belt on his robe and fumbled with the ties. When it fell free, she shoved it off of his shoulders. The heavy velvet made a soft thump as it hit the floor behind him.

Gabriel cupped the back of her neck and deepened the kiss again. Their tongues tangled and dueled. There were no games with his Lily. No coy looks and empty teasing. Only passion. Honest need that set his body aflame. She met his kisses with a matching hunger he'd rarely felt before. He'd had hundreds of passionate nights with his various lovers. But this…this was different. The hunger, the need, was more intense.

He licked her neck and pressed hot kisses down her throat while the fingers of his free hand quested for the open vee of fair skin beneath his mouth. He traced the edge of her night rail, flipped aside the ribbon she hadn't tied to keep it closed, and dipped his fingers under the material.

Lily undulated against him.

"Yes," she panted. "Touch me, Gabriel."

He would. He wouldn't stop until she came apart beneath his hands and his tongue.

His fingers traced the edge of her nipple.

Lily sucked in a breath which teased that delightful bud away from his touch.

"No," he murmured against her neck. "Don't run, my love."

He dipped his hand further beneath her gown. The moment his palm brushed her nipple, a muffled thump and a pained yelp came from outside the door.

Gabriel's need was so great that he almost didn't release her. Only her surprised squeak and the gentle shove at his shoulders made him step back. Letting go of that perfect, heavy breast was going to haunt his dreams.

Lily slipped off of the table and picked up some of the books that had fallen onto the floor.

He reached for his dressing gown and nearly moaned. His cock was so hard that it hurt. He wanted Lily to pull him into a shadowed corner and wrap her hand around it. Or her mouth.

The person in the hallway cursed and then a door closed.

One look at Lily's face told him the moment had passed. *Damn.*

She grabbed the first book within reach and pressed it to her chest that rose and fell in rapid pants. At least she'd been as affected as he. He felt bewitched.

"I, uh...should...goodnight, Gabriel." She edged around him and slipped out the door.

He squeezed the back of his neck and closed his eyes. *Blast.* Lily Bennett had just given him the best kiss of his life.

CHAPTER EIGHT

"ROTHDEN, ARE YOU going to take your turn or brood all day?" Noah Cradock shoved a billiards cue at him, wrenching his gaze away from the window overlooking the path that wound toward the woods behind the house.

"He's still upset about missing the hunt," Granville said.

Gabriel huffed and lined up his shot. The red ball sank into the pocket. They were playing billiards while the ladies enjoyed their time in the drawing room, playing cards, writing correspondence, or reading.

"Blast." Noah tossed his stick at Granville and fished a farthing out of his pocket. He dropped it in Granville's waiting palm. "Even when he's distracted, he wins."

Had she slept well after leaving the library last night? Dreamed of him? He scrubbed a hand down his face. He'd been so aroused from their encounter, he'd had to take himself in hand once he returned to his room. That small release did little to cool his ardor. He'd spent the rest of the night listening for sounds of her in the next room and listing all the reasons that he shouldn't use the connecting door between their chambers.

As a result, he'd barely slept, and that always made him grumpy. The damn falling rain outside only heightened his mood. Maybe if it had been a sunny day, he could have gone for a long ride. Hell, even a walk. But the blasted weather kept him indoors. Closer to the woman who consumed his thoughts. It was madness. He didn't know her well enough to want her like this. Sadly, his body didn't seem to give a whit.

"*Rothden.*"

Cradock speared him with a look that said he'd called his name a couple times.

Gabriel arched a brow.

Christian chuckled from where he sat by the window, with a handkerchief in one hand and some scrap of red in the other.

He shot his friend a look, but Christian's lips twitched. His face said he had an inkling where Gabriel's mind had wandered. The man had been there for the dance lessons, after all.

"Are you playing the next game?" Cradock asked.

"No." Gabriel handed off his cue stick to Somersby. "You've given enough of your money to Granville for one day."

"Nonsense, I can fit much more in my pocket," Granville said.

Seabright pointed his cigar at Somersby. "Don't lose."

Somersby scoffed. "Against Cradock? I could beat him faster than Rothden."

"Only because the man's distracted. Probably by some bit of skirt if I know that look," Twisden said as he filled a glass of brandy from the sideboard. "Care to share who, Rothden?"

Gabriel narrowed his eyes. As if he'd say a word to Twisden. The man had looser lips than a dowager at a ball.

Reginald appeared in the doorway and interrupted Gabriel's reply. "My lord, a carriage comes up the drive."

"I'm not expecting anyone." Maybe it was the doctor, returning to check on Lily. "If you'll excuse me, gentlemen."

He followed Reginald into the hall. The front door opened, and a chilly gust of rain blew into the entry. His butler held the door open as a woman entered.

Rothden stopped mid-stride. He'd know those curves anywhere. At one time, he couldn't get enough of her soft, full breasts and perfect arse. His pulse quickened, but not in pleasure. His jaw tensed.

"Lady Caroline Montrose," Reginald announced, sounding as enthused about their newest arrival as Gabriel felt.

Lady Montrose sauntered through the door, swaying her hips and puffing her breasts out. She gave him a slow smile that just curved her mouth. A pout she'd perfected over the years. Her blonde hair was set in perfect ringlets under a blue bonnet with feathers and ribbon trim. It matched her travel habit, which fit her bodice snuggly to show off her every curve.

"My darling, Rothden," she cooed as she came toward him with her hands extended. "You must have thought me terribly rude for not arriving on time or sending word. My invitation must have been lost by the post. Can you imagine?"

Gabriel bowed over one of her hands. Once, he would have brushed his lips over the back of her glove, allowing them to linger. Now, he hesitated to touch her at all. He had no wish to encourage her affections in any way she might misconstrue as interest. "Lady Montrose."

She removed her cloak, thrusting it at Reginald.

The old steward tilted his large nose in the air and sniffed. He pinched the garment between two fingers as if it had been dredged from the bottom of the Thames, and handed it to the butler.

"You must tell me everything that I've missed. Did you have a hunting party? If so, I do hope you'll arrange another. You know how much I love them. Hopefully the weather will improve. Can you believe this rain?"

Gabriel drew a deep breath and used the moment to rein in his irritation. At the end of the Season three months past, he'd ended their arrangement in as plain a speech as he could. Caroline had been his mistress for just over a year. She'd been a wild lover in bed. Totally uninhibited. It drew his passions from the start, and the flame burned bright. But as often happens with a burst of fire, it soon faded. Her attempts to gain his attention became needy and grasping, and her love of salacious gossip made her seem petty and jealous. In short order, he'd grown bored. It had taken three months more to release himself from her claws. Fool that he was, he'd thought she would move on. Her presence here quite clearly stated otherwise.

"Caroline…" he began. If she turned around now, she could make the first inn before nightfall.

"Dear Reginald, would you be so kind as to have my trunk taken up to my normal room beside Rothden's?"

Reginald's dark eyebrows rose, and he met Gabriel's gaze in an unspoken question. Was the lady staying?

"Oh, you must see it, Patience," Violet said as the two women walked out of the drawing room. "I had the gown made as soon as my brother approved the masked ball. And the matching mask…you've never seen anything so lovely in—" She paused when she spotted Caroline in the entry. Her eyes narrowed.

Damn. He'd been about to turn Caroline away. Now that he had an audience, social decorum held his tongue. Slighting her in front of others could have disastrous consequence for himself and Violet. People would sympathize with Caroline as the victim, and he would be relegated to the same esteem as the devil himself. Worse, it could potentially harm Violet's chances for a good match.

Although now that he considered it, the idea had merit.

Damn! No, he loved his sister. He wouldn't ruin her chance at happiness by evicting his unwanted ex-mistress from his house party. It was only another week. He would suffer through.

Gabriel gave a slight nod to Reginald.

The steward curled his lip in distaste. Then a look of pure devilry crossed his face. He pasted on the brightest smile Gabriel had ever seen on the man.

"I deeply regret to inform you, Lady Montrose, but that chamber is taken by the *delightful* Miss Lily Bennett at my lord's direction. I'm afraid she is staying for quite some time."

He pinched the bridge of his nose at his steward's gleeful tone. He feigned a frown, but internally, he wanted to laugh at the old coot.

"What?" Caroline demanded. "But you knew I would be here. How dare you give my room to another?"

"Forgive me, my lady. But when you didn't arrive with the other guests, it was believed that you'd decided against attending the house party. That perhaps your decline was lost by the *post*." Reginald's eyes crinkled when he smiled at her.

Caroline glared at Reginald, then turned a shade of red as she swung around to no doubt say something biting to Gabriel. She spotted Violet and Patience in the entry, staring with interest. Caroline smoothed her features. "Oh…these things happen. I do hope there is another chamber available?"

"Certainly," Gabriel said before Reginald could offer up a drafty attic space or the servant's quarters. "I believe there is an empty bedroom at the other end of the hall. Reginald, if you would please have the room prepared for the lady?"

Reginald looked as mutinous as Violet often did, but nodded and directed the footmen to bring the lady's trunk up to the room.

Gabriel turned to find the same look on his sister's face. He sighed. "Violet, perhaps you and Patience will introduce Lady Montrose to the other women and ring for tea?"

Violet glared at him. "I'd be delighted," she said through clenched teeth. "Lady Montrose?" She waved her hand toward the drawing room.

Caroline pressed her lips together in a tight smile.

"I shall join you as soon as I see to your comfort," he said. His words seemed to mollify her. Caroline swept through the entry and entered the drawing room.

Violet propped her fists on her hips and loudly whispered, "What about Lily?"

Christ. He didn't want to think about Caroline anywhere near Lily. "It's only a few more days, Vi." He wasn't sure if he was trying to convince her or himself. But a sickening turn of his stomach told him that Caroline's arrival would not offer the peaceful interlude between friends that he'd hoped for. So far, nothing had. Perhaps he ought to return to London for the respite he needed. Surely the noisy, foul-smelling streets would offer more relaxation than his house party currently did.

COULD A PERSON be considered a wallflower if they never left their bedroom to go to the dance? Lily pressed her hands over her stomach to stop the flutter of rioting butterflies and drew a deep breath. The butterflies doubled, breeding like rabbits.

Gabriel taught me the steps. I won't step on any feet or trip over the train on my gown and fall flat on my face. It'll be fine.

She swallowed. Right. She could do this.

Lily took one last look in the mirror, admiring the burgundy evening gown she'd borrowed from Violet. The underdress was made of burgundy satin, with a high waist and puffed sleeves. A black velvet ribbon with a ruby and pearl brooch ran under the bust, accentuating the snug fit. Fine burgundy lace covered most of the bodice and skirt, parting down the center to reveal the satin beneath and trailed out in a mini train. A maid had curled and pinned up her hair, adding a few burgundy ribbons and flowers.

Despite her nerves, she'd never felt prettier. A small smile curled her lips. What would Gabriel think of her in this gown? Would he want to kiss her again?

His kisses in the library two nights ago filled her dreams. God, it was the best kiss she'd ever had. He'd kissed her hungrily. In moments, the attraction she felt for him had burst into an inferno that burned her from the inside out. She still remembered the feel of his skin beneath her fingers, her lips. If it hadn't been for the loud clatter of something falling in the hall, Lily would have begged him to take her right there. It was that realization that had sent her scurrying to her room. She didn't have sex with a man the first time she kissed him. But Gabriel's kisses addled her mind until all that remained was the need to rip his clothes off and taste all of that tawny skin.

Lily swiped up her lace fan and flicked it open, cooling her heated cheeks. If just the thought of his kisses made her burn, what would it feel like if they did more?

Violet chose that moment to knock once and sail into her room. "I thought I would find you here. Lily, the dance has started. Quit mooning about and come downstairs. You'll dazzle all of the men and won't step on a single toe." She looped her arm through Lily's and towed her toward the door.

"How do you always know what I'm worried about?"

Violet laughed. "Because it's what I worried about when I first learned to dance." They paused at the top of the stairs, and Violet's gaze turned inward. "Christian was my first dance partner. I was too afraid to accept any other offer, and even though he despises balls and crowds and dancing, he insisted on a dance. It was a wonderful night, and I'll always be grateful to him."

Lily had sat beside him at dinner most evenings and enjoyed trying to coax him into a conversation. Underneath the genius lay a soft heart. She hoped one day that a woman would burrow her way beneath Christian's somewhat social awkwardness to see the special man beneath.

They descended the stairs to the first floor where the gentle strains of music flowed out of the open salon doors. The butler greeted them at the door and announced them.

Violet must have sensed her hesitation creeping back in because she gave her a gentle shove into the room. Lily shot her a dark look. Violet flashed her impish smile in response, then took her arm and together they threaded through the crowd of people.

The salon was painted a pretty light blue, trimmed with cream woodwork. Candlelight flickered in the chandeliers above, and the windows were cracked to let in a bit of cool night air. Most of the furniture had been removed, except for a few chairs for the dowager ladies. In addition to the house party guests, a number of couples from the village and surrounding countryside were in attendance. There had to be at least fifty people. A small quartet of musicians sat in one corner of the room, playing a tune as guests mingled.

Lily scanned the group, hoping to see Gabriel. Christian leaned against a wall in navy blue coat tails, looking miserable. Zeph, the enigmatic man with the white-blond hair stood beside him, a slight smile on his face. He often wore the same look of mischief as Violet did.

The last house party guest to arrive, Lady Montrose, stood in a circle of five men. She wore a dark blue gown that accented her lithe frame and a glittering sapphire necklace. As she spoke, her hand fluttered at her chest, not quite touching it. The men surrounding her seemed enraptured.

"Oh, there's Lord Musgrave," Violet said a bit breathlessly. "I'll ask him to get us some punch." She nearly skipped toward him in a flurry of green taffeta, a bright smile on her face.

"He knows better than to have designs on my sister," a low voice growled behind her.

Lily turned to find Gabriel glowering at his friend. She laughed. "But does Violet know better than to have designs on him?"

He muttered a dark curse. "She will." Gabriel looked down at her and stilled. His gaze drifted down over her dress, lingering on her breasts only a moment before finding their way back up. "You're beautiful. No spectacles this evening?"

"I thought it would be better if I couldn't see the look on people's faces if I trip and fall."

He snorted. "Wise, but unnecessary. You dance gracefully, Lily. You have nothing to worry over."

It warmed her heart that he thought so, even if she still had doubts. He was so handsome in his black coat tails and embroidered gold waistcoat. His white cravat, tied to perfection, brought out his skin and dark hair.

"We will start with a quadrille tonight. Would you grant me the honor of the first dance?" He held out a gloved hand.

Lily set her hand in his and allowed him to lead her toward the dance floor. The music changed to a tune she recognized as the melody that Patience had played as Gabriel taught her the quadrille. One side of Gabriel's mouth curled as he looked at her from the corner of his eye and gave her a slight nod. She set her shoulders back, feeling a new confidence.

More couples joined them on the dance floor, including Violet and Lord Musgrave, and the dance began. Gabriel guided her easily through the turns, weaving in and out of the other dancers. Lily laughed in delight when his eyes twinkled at her as they came together, then danced apart, and at last, her fears faded.

She danced several more times, including a gallopade with Lord Twisden that left her breathless. Unfortunately, she hadn't had a chance to dance with Gabriel again after the quadrille. Every time she looked for him, she found him with Lady Montrose. The woman leaned closer to him every time she spoke. Any closer, and she could drape herself over the man like a blanket.

Lily accepted a second cup of punch from Lord Musgrave. She thanked him, but her words were lost as he focused on Violet beside her. She stepped away to give them a bit of privacy. Not that there was much privacy to be had in the crowded salon. She drifted along the edge of the crowd until she was at the window closest to the door, savoring the crisp air on her heated skin.

The faint scent of pine hit her a moment before Gabriel's husky voice spoke into her ear.

"Are you enjoying yourself, love?"

She shivered and turned her head to look up at him. He towered over her, so near that he almost pressed to her back. A different kind of heat washed over her, tightening her nipples. "Very much."

He looked at her lips, then met her gaze. "I came to ask you for another dance. Instead, I think perhaps we should take in some air." He tucked her hand into his arm. As people moved to the dance floor for another quadrille, Gabriel took advantage of their distraction and pulled her out of the salon into the darkened hallway.

"Where are we going?" she asked.

Gabriel's lips twitched. He ushered her down the short corridor and into an alcove with a landscape painting and a plinth with a marble bust. Shadows enveloped them. He spun her into his arms and pulled her against his chest. "I quite like the air here, don't you?"

Her core tightened, and her breath caught. Lily put her hands on his chest, feeling the beat of his heart. It matched the hard thump of her own. "I do. It smells like you."

He uttered a soft growl and lowered his mouth, capturing her lips in that hungry kiss that made her knees weak. Lily wound her arms around his neck and opened to his tongue.

She lost herself in his hot kiss and the strength of his arms. Kissing Gabriel was unlike kissing anyone else. She never wanted to leave. When his mouth was on hers, she didn't worry about the future or finding a way back to her own time. She didn't feel lonely or like a failure for being unable to keep her family together.

Lily broke the kiss and stared up at him. Kissing Gabriel felt like home. Like safety and warmth and love all rolled into one. The feeling scared her. It made her want to stay in England.

He cupped her cheek and feathered his thumb over her skin. "You did well dancing. No one would know you only recently learned. Would you join me for the next dance? I believe there will be a waltz soon."

Lily nodded.

"Perhaps tomorrow we might go for a ride in the park? I want to hear more about your world. About you."

Her heart warmed again. "I'd like that."

His thumb brushed her lower lip. "Would you—"

A low cough sounded nearby. "Lord Rothden, the local constable is here to see you."

Gabriel groaned. "Hang it all, Reginald. Must you lurk nearby?"

"I don't lurk," the steward sniffed.

He released a long sigh. "What does the man want?"

"I'm sure I don't know. Shall I lurk around the front door for you? Or would you prefer to meet the man as he is requesting?"

Gabriel's jaw ticked. To Lily he said, "I will find you for our dance once this is settled." He brushed his lips over her temple, then spun to stalk down the hall.

Lily followed a few moments later and slipped into the salon. As she moved through the crowd of people, leaving the dance floor between songs, the back of her neck prickled. She turned to find Lady Montrose standing a few feet away, staring at her.

"Even in a country dance with only a few couples, I suppose one still needs to get some air," the woman said. Her tone sounded congenial, but a cold light swept through her blue eyes.

"I'm not used to dances like this," Lily replied when the woman smiled. Had she imagined the look of anger and jealousy?

"Of course. How silly of me. I imagine it has been ages since you spent time in civilized company." Lady Montrose slipped her arm through Lily's and guided her toward Lord Somersby, who stood at the edge of the dance floor. She raised her voice to be heard above the din of conversation. "I have a wonderful idea. You and Lord Somersby should lead us in the next dance. How about a Scottish reel?"

"Delightful!" Somersby said and bowed over Lily's hand. "Will you join me, Miss Bennett?"

Lily swallowed. The Scottish reel wasn't one of the dances that Gabriel taught her. She certainly couldn't lead it. She pulled her shaking hand out of Somersby's light hold. "I'm sorry, Lord Somersby. Maybe later."

Caroline smiled, sweet layered over the grin of a hungry snake. "Not quite enough air? You do look pale. Perhaps you should retire for the evening. I'm certain Rothden won't miss your presence."

Somersby's brow furrowed as he looked between them. "I believe Miss Bennett would indeed be missed."

Lily didn't know what to say. The woman's words hit the bullseye on her insecurities. She felt awkward and out of place, with Somersby looking at her expectantly and Lady Montrose's superior posture. She excused herself. When she turned, a few of the dowager ladies were huddled nearby, watching her. She ducked her head as she passed.

"I heard she's an *American*," one whispered. "I'm surprised that Lord Rothden would have someone so unseemly in attendance."

"No wonder she's on the shelf. She probably doesn't remember how to dance because it's been so long since someone asked," another said in a louder voice meant to carry. They laughed. "I heard Lady Montrose say that she's hoping Lord Rothden might make their arrangement more of a permanent nature."

"If so, I imagine she would put an end to inviting unsuitable young women to events such as this," the first replied.

Lily turned to slide around a few gentlemen, hoping to get out of earshot, when someone stepped on the train of her gown. She stumbled a step forward but managed to right herself. Someone chuckled nearby. She lifted the trailing gown off the floor and squeezed out of the crowd. At the door to the salon, she looked back.

Caroline led the dance with Somersby flawlessly.

She shouldn't let those women get to her. She knew that. But it wasn't so much what they said but how it made her feel—awkward and insecure. It reminded her that while she might look the part and know some of the etiquette, she didn't belong here. This wasn't her world, and it never would be.

Lily needed to find a way home.

CHAPTER NINE

W HERE THE DEVIL was Lily? He'd been caught in a conversation with the local constable about the theft of a horse from the neighboring farm. It was nearing midnight, and many of his guests would leave soon. Such parties ended earlier in the country than in London, where the Ton liked to stay well into the night. He wanted one last dance with her.

He searched through the guests in the salon first, then stalked through the door. Perhaps she'd slipped away to the retiring room.

Violet waited for him on the other side. She paced the small entry with her arms folded over her chest. The moment she spotted him, she stomped up to him and poked him in the chest. "Lily was quite upset, Gabriel. I thought you said that your *mistress* wasn't invited."

"She wasn't." He captured her finger and held it away.

Violet poked him with a finger from her other hand. "How odd, because it seems that she is here gracing us all with her presence."

He grabbed for that hand, and they ended up in a minor tussle. He swore. "Vi!"

She yanked her hands away. "She embarrassed Lily, Gabriel. In front of half of the guests."

"I ended our arrangement at the end of the Season, as I told you, and I did not invite her. How she came to know of the party is immaterial. She is here. Rest assured that if she continues to cause mischief, then I will send her away."

"You promise?"

He took her hand, this time in a gentle grip and placed his other hand atop it. "Violet, I would never intentionally put Lily in a situation that would embarrass her. If Caroline cannot behave with the kindness that I know she is capable of, then I will not allow her to stay."

She wound her arms around his waist. "Thank you, Gabriel. I know we've only known Lily a few short days, but I like her. Seeing her upset made me want to rip Lady Montrose's hair out. More than usual, I mean."

He pressed his cheek to the top of her head. "If she is unkind to Lily again, you have my permission."

Violet chuckled against his chest. "Will you talk to Lily? She's in her room."

"Yes. Now, enjoy the last few dances. And don't trip Lady Montrose during a quadrille."

She huffed as if put upon, then pressed a kiss to his cheek, and returned to the salon.

He hurried up the stairs and stopped before Lily's door, listening. Was that a slight snuffle? Blast. He was making a habit of lurking outside her chamber like Reginald skulked outside whatever room he was in.

Gabriel knocked on the door before someone saw him standing there like a fool. "Miss Bennett? Lily? May I come in? I... would like to speak to you."

A shuffle, a sniff, and a moment later, the door opened. She still wore the beautiful gown, but she'd removed her gloves. A few glossy brown curls had escaped her hair pins, and her eyes were red and wet. She leaned her head against the door. "Hi, Gabr—"

He swept her up against his chest before the words left her mouth and kicked the door closed. Seeing her tears undid him. He hated when any woman cried, but Lily's tears felt like they tugged out his heart. He cursed Caroline anew.

Lily clutched his shoulders and gasped as he strode to the chair by the fire and sat, nestling her into his lap. She looked at him with wide eyes.

"I'm sorry for what happened tonight, Lily. I should have turned her away the moment she arrived, but my concern was for Violet's reputation this coming Season."

She sniffled and breathed deep. "Lady Montrose is…your mistress? Your lover?"

He wrapped his arms a little tighter around her waist. "She was, but no longer. I ended the relationship several months back. I thought she would move on."

"I don't think she has." Lily clasped her hands in her lap and looked at her fingers. "Not that I blame her. I think you would be very hard to let go."

His heart picked up speed. "You don't know me that well, Lily. I could snore loud enough to bring down the roof."

"I think I would have heard you through the connecting door."

She knew the door led to his bedroom? The thought of having her that close made his blood heat. "I could have buried the bodies of my enemies in the forest behind my house."

"Violet would be more likely to do that." She paused and leaned back. "Are you… are you trying to keep me from liking you?" Lily tried to scramble out of his lap, but he clamped his arms around her and held her in place.

"No. On the contrary, I hope that you do like me. Because I find that I quite like you, Lily." He tucked a loose curl behind her ear.

She searched his face. "I do. I like the way you banter with Violet. I can see how much you love her. I like the way you care about your friends and the people who work for you. Even strangers who show up on your doorstep from another century. A few bodies buried in the backyard won't take away from that."

He chuckled and shifted her until she pressed against his chest. "I'll remind you of that if Caroline is missing tomorrow."

Lily smiled, and the room lit up with her. "Thank you, Gabriel. I shouldn't have let her get to me. She just hit all the right buttons, you know?"

He tilted his head.

"I mean, she knew just what to say to upset me. She's a lot like my sister in that regard. Her knife stabbed at the heart of my insecurities."

Gabriel pressed a kiss to her soft cheek. "She is insecure also, Lily. Caroline fears that if she isn't the most beautiful, accomplished woman in the room, that people will gossip and spread cruel words about her. Tonight, your beauty shone brighter, and she was jealous."

She traced the knot of his cravat.

When she didn't respond, he swept away the last of the moisture from her cheek. Thank God she wasn't crying anymore. Those tears gutted him. This woman reached him on levels no others had, leaving him feeling both unsettled and teetering on the brink of something important.

"Lily," he whispered.

She met his gaze.

"I'm going to kiss you again."

She nodded, and released the breath he didn't realize that he was holding. With all the gentleness he could muster, he cupped her neck and drew her lips to his. He kissed her softly, savoring the satin touch of her mouth. This was different than the kiss they'd shared in the library, but no less passionate.

Lily moaned and pressed closer. She wound her arms around his neck and slanted her head, seeking more.

Gabriel licked her lips, encouraging her to open for him. He explored the sweet depths of her mouth, stroking her tongue with his. All thoughts of his guests were forgotten. Only Lily remained.

She wiggled in his lap. He broke the kiss, intending to release her.

Instead, she hiked up her skirts and straddled his lap, then speared her fingers into his hair and pulled his lips back to hers.

The kiss caught fire, making him burn. He met her mouth hungrily, sucking her bottom lip, stroking her tongue.

Lily moaned into his mouth. She rocked her hips and gasped when she brushed against his hard cock. She pulled her mouth away, staring into his eyes.

Gabriel mustered up an apology, but before he could get it past his lips, she was kissing him harder. She cupped his cheeks, nibbled his bottom lip, and rubbed her heat against him.

She felt amazing in his arms. He needed more. Gabriel kissed over her jaw and down her neck, savoring the sweetness of her skin. He smelled the soap from her bath and underneath, the honey of her skin. He tasted her there, licking the tender line of her throat.

She shivered. "More, Gabriel." She pushed his hands beneath his tailcoat and pushed it off of his shoulders. "I want to feel you."

He shrugged out of his coat and yanked at the knot of his cravat. Felt her fingers working the buttons of his waistcoat open. Then she was pulling his linen shirt out of his trousers. Suddenly, her hands were on his bare chest, and Gabriel moaned.

Lily pressed a kiss to the skin of his throat.

He tilted his head against the back of the chair and dragged air into his lungs. "I want to touch you, too."

"Yes. Please Gabriel. Touch me."

She placed one of his hands over her breast and the other at the spot where the hiked-up hem of her skirt met her leg.

She's perfect. He cupped her heavy breast through the bodice of her gown, wishing she was naked in his arms. Lily leaned into his touch. He stroked his thumb over her hardening nipple while his other hand shoved the gown and petticoats out of the way until he could feel her smooth thigh above her stockings. Her skin was like silk.

She rocked her hips over his cock and moaned at the friction.

"Does that feel good, love? Do you like rubbing yourself against me?"

"Yes," she hissed as she circled her hips.

"Let me make you feel even better."

She gently bit his bottom lip. "Please, Gabriel."

He slid his hand up her silky inner thigh to cup her heat. Wetness met his fingers, and he stroked through her folds. He hummed in appreciation. "You're slick for me."

Lily sat back and reached behind her, struggling for the ties of her dress.

"Allow me, love." Gabriel helped her to her feet and spun her around. He pressed a lingering kiss to the base of her neck, then made quick work of her laces. With a few tugs, her dress pooled at her feet. He unlaced her stays, and helped her out of her petticoat, leaving her only in a thin shift and stockings. He gently pulled the pins from her hair until a mass of thick, honey and caramel curls fell past her shoulders.

Lily turned in his arms and helped divest him of his waistcoat and shirt. His cravat and coat were already on the floor. He didn't give a whit.

Gabriel returned to the chair and pulled Lily back into his lap. She raised her shift enough to straddle him. Only his trousers separated her wet heat from his shaft.

She kissed him, softly at first, and then harder. Once more, she put his hand onto her breast. "Touch me, Gabriel."

Her hard nipple abraded his palm through the thin linen. Gabriel cupped both of her breasts, feeling the weight in his palms and squeezing them gently. He brushed his thumbs over her peaks, feeling them grow stiff with his ministrations. Dear God, he had to taste her. He bent his head and sucked a nipple into his mouth, circling his tongue over the fabric, using the material to stimulate her.

Lily ground her hips and cried out. She pulled at the neckline of the shift, trying to lower it.

Gabriel lifted his head. The golden glow of the fireplace set her hair aflame and highlighted the sweet curves of her body in the darkened room. "Lily," he whispered.

She pressed a tender kiss to his lips, then worked the shift off one shoulder and then the other.

He couldn't help but stare. A plentiful bosom was his weakness when it came to women. Her breasts were full, with rosy, pink nipples on milky skin. They budded hard beneath his gaze. He lowered his head and took her into his mouth. Flicked his tongue back and forth over one hard nipple and then the other. He lost himself in the feel of her, the taste.

Lily rocked against him, making him even harder, until he thought his cock might pop the buttons on his trousers.

He reached beneath her shift and stroked her wet opening. She shuddered in his arms, and her head fell back. Dear God, she was beautiful. He stroked through her folds, back and forth, then added his thumb to rub circles around one hard nub.

"Will you come for me, my sweet Lily?" he murmured against her breast. "Will you come apart in my arms and show me your ecstasy?"

She moaned.

"Is that a yes, love?"

Lily nodded, but no words left her lips.

He switched to suck on her other breast, increasing the speed of his thumb. Between her thighs, he found her entrance and slid one finger inside. Her hips circled, seeking the right friction. "That's right. Take what you need."

Lily plunged her hands into his hair and gripped tightly. She shivered.

"Let go, love," he murmured.

Her eyes met his, and then her inner walls clamped down on his finger, and she came with a husky cry.

Gabriel had never seen anything so beautiful in his entire life. He helped her slowly descend from her orgasm, until she sagged against his chest, breathing heavy. He pressed a kiss to the top of her head and tried to rein in his lust. A few more moments of her grinding on his cock and he would release right there.

"That was amazing," she said.

He removed his hand from between her thighs. Holding her gaze, he licked his fingers. "Mmm. Delicious."

She trembled and kissed him. "I… I like the taste of myself on your lips."

Gabriel groaned. It took all of his willpower not to lay her out on the bed and bring her to an orgasm with his mouth so she could taste more.

Her hands lowered to his trouser buttons. "Can I…?"

He caught her hands. "I fear if I have any more of you tonight, I won't let you out of my bed for days. My guests will most definitely note my absence."

She tilted her head as if she was considering the consequences.

Gabriel chuckled and pressed a sweet kiss to her lips. He helped her pull her shift back into place, covering up those luscious breasts.

"Raincheck?" she asked.

He arched an eyebrow.

"It means, will you give me an opportunity in the future to give you pleasure?"

"You don't have to."

"I want to, Gabriel. I want to make you feel as good as you make me feel."

He cupped her cheek. "You already do." The moment stretched between them. It wasn't an uncomfortable silence. Instead, it felt…charged. Like words were spoken between their bodies. Their souls.

Fanciful nonsense, he chided himself. Yet he couldn't let the thought go.

>>><<<

"IF MEN NO longer take women on picnics after they get married, then perhaps I don't want a husband after all," Violet said as she set her teacup in its saucer on the picnic blanket. Her curls were pinned up under a bonnet sporting a purple ribbon that matched her violet walking gown.

"Don't be a ninny, Violet," Patience said. "If your husband doesn't take you on a picnic, then you go with your friends, like we did." She tugged her shawl closer and reached for a cucumber sandwich.

"Or you take *him* for a picnic," Lily added.

Violet burst into giggles. "That is *exactly* what I shall do."

After two days of rain and a chilly wind, the sun was out, adding a little more warmth to the autumn air. Bright red and yellow leaves clung valiantly to tree branches, while the rest fell to the grass in a pretty patchwork of color. A perfect day for a picnic, Violet had declared that morning. She'd ordered a lunch packed and set about ushering Lily and Patience into a carriage to enjoy the sunshine.

They now sat on a large blanket in the village park, surrounded by half a dozen colorful pillows for reclining and multiple picnic baskets. To Lily, it felt more like an outdoor dinner party than a picnic. They used painted China plates and silverware, poured tea from a China teapot, and drank from real cups and saucers. Lunch was an enormous selection of sandwiches, scones with clotted cream and jam, little tea cakes, blueberries and blackberries, cheeses and breads. Far more food than just the three of them could eat.

Gabriel and his guests had taken advantage of the weather and scheduled a second hunt, leaving the women behind. Except for Lady Montrose.

Lily couldn't decide if she was pleased to not have to endure the woman's company or unsettled that the woman would be in Gabriel's company all day. Not that Lily had any hold on Gabriel or who he chose to spend time with. But after their make-out session…

"What a lovely flush you have, Lily. Whatever are you thinking of to bring about such color?" Violet asked with an impish twinkle.

Lily took a bite of pastry to avoid the question and smoothed a hand over her skirt. She wore her new, green walking dress with a bonnet she'd borrowed from Violet with tiny sprigs of white silk flowers on it.

"Maybe she's a little warm under the sun," Patience said.

"Don't be a silly goose, Patience. My brother is fond of Lily. If he stole a kiss, I want to know all about it."

"You want to know how your brother kisses, Violet? How sordid." Patience grinned and winked at Lily.

Violet reached for the nearest pillow and whacked her friend, toppling over a plate of finger sandwiches.

Patience squawked and tossed the pillow back.

Lily laughed. She couldn't remember the last time she'd had such fun with girlfriends. She…she didn't really have any at home. Not since her parents had died.

"Many of my friends have been smitten with my brother. I have spent hours listening to their wishful ponderings of what it would be like to wed him. Of course, he's too smart to steal a kiss from them, lest he find himself in the marriage trap. He's preferred women like that dreadful Lady Montrose." Violet made a face. She looked at Lily. "But he's different with you. I saw him follow you last night, Lily."

The unspoken question lingered in the air.

Patience leaned forward. "Did he kiss you?"

Did Gabriel kiss her? No, he *devoured* her. She shivered and held back a little moan. She'd never come so hard in her life. Her old boyfriend had never taken her body to such heights. The chemistry between them scorched her, and the sensual promise in Gabriel's eyes stole her breath. It took all of her willpower not to drop to her knees in front of him despite his claim that the pleasure was only for her. Lily wanted to put her mouth on him. In fact, she wanted a lot more. But there were so many complications to giving in to that desire.

What if she were only a passing fancy to Gabriel? What if she went home? God, what if she stayed? She couldn't risk her heart again, only to find him kissing someone else.

"Lily?" Violet called.

She realized that they were still waiting for her to acknowledge whether or not she'd kissed Gabriel. She realized then that she could hold all these feelings and doubts in, or she could open up and talk to these women who were quickly becoming friends.

I want to have friends again.

"Gabriel gave me the best kiss I've ever had," she admitted softly. There were some things that she wouldn't share, obviously. Like how good he was with his tongue in places other than her mouth.

Patience grinned.

Violet hooted in triumph. "I knew he liked you. Will you become my sister-in-law?"

Lily choked on a sip of tea. "Violet! What if…" her gaze skated to Patience. "What if I go home?"

"You can't go home. Wait, have you figured out how to get home?" Violet's dark brows drew together. "Tell me you haven't."

"Why would you not know how to get home? Or is there a problem with passage to America?" Patience asked.

Lily hadn't found anything in the library about clocks. She was no closer to learning who made the clock as she was to finding out why she appeared where she had or even how she traveled through time in the first place. She could be stuck here for good.

"Would it be so bad to be 'stuck' with us?" Violet asked.

Lily hadn't realized she'd spoken aloud. "No. Yes. I don't know. I mean, if I do stay, what will I do?"

"Marry my brother," Violet said as if the answer was obvious to everyone but Lily.

"Your brother is an earl, Violet. Even if he does like me, I can't be more than a passing interest to him. I'm only someone a little different than what he's used to."

"Pish. I've only just met you, and even I know that you are a diamond of the first water," Patience said. "Gabriel would be lucky to land you as a wife."

Lily rubbed her eyes. How could she make them understand? There couldn't be a future between her and Gabriel. They made it sound like he would drop to his knee tomorrow to propose. "That's not how life works," she muttered. "That's not how *my* life works anyway. Men like Gabriel move on to the next beautiful woman all the time."

She held up a hand when Violet started to protest. "I've been down that road. Mason broke my heart. I can't go through that again."

"Who is Mason?" Patience asked.

"He was my boyfriend. My beau. He was handsome and charming. Very popular with women like Gabriel is. I should have known. I mean, he was a singer in a band. There were going to be groupies. But I really thought he liked me. That maybe he didn't introduce me to his friends because he wanted to keep me all to himself." It sounded idiotic when she said the words aloud. Men only did that in romance novels.

"I found him kissing another woman. A prettier one."

Violet's hand covered hers, drawing her out of her thoughts. "If he kissed another woman, he didn't deserve you."

"Don't many men take mistresses even when they're married?" God, she couldn't live with that.

Patience hummed. "Some. Noah says that no mistress could ever make him as happy as I have."

Violet elbowed her. "We'll talk about your kisses next."

Lily felt a warmth in her heart for these women that she hadn't felt in some time. "Even so, I don't think there can be anything serious between Gabriel and me."

Violet's chin lifted. "We'll see."

They finished their picnic, and several footmen came from where the carriage waited to pack up the food and dishes. Next, they strolled along the shops and stopped at the modiste to pick up the rest of Lily's wardrobe.

"The carriage is going to be so overloaded that we'll have to walk back," Lily said as one of the men loaded a fifth package onto the carriage. "The horses won't be able to pull all of that weight."

Patience laughed. "In that case, I volunteer Violet to walk since it was her idea that we have a picnic and pick up your wardrobe on the same day."

"Do you see that?" Violet asked as she looked down the lane.

Lily followed her gaze and saw a Hawthorne footman descend from another carriage. Before she could ask why that would be unusual, Violet hurried toward him.

CHAPTER TEN

AUTUMN BROUGHT CRISP days and a colorful carpet of leaves to the woods at Hawthorne. Oak, sycamore, and walnut trees lifted their steady limbs to the bright blue sky above. After a bit of rain, the air smelled fresh and clean. A perfect day for a hunt.

Gabriel sat astride his Irish Hunter, patting the dark gray horse's neck. His hunting dogs sniffed the ground ahead, running in zigzags, searching for grouse. Their party of ten rode through the forest on his estate and along the meadows. Caroline had elected to join them. When she wasn't riding beside him, trying to engage him in conversation, she rode between Twisden and Granville. He hoped to God she'd stay there.

Christian rode up beside him. His cravat was loose as if he'd been tugging on it and dark finger smudges marred his buckskin trousers. "Tell me you aren't wishing you were on a picnic right now."

A muscle in his jaw ticked and he scowled at his friend. Hang it all, he couldn't, and Christian knew it. He blew out a noisy breath. "I hope the ladies enjoy themselves today."

Christian's lip quirked on one side. "Hunting has been one of your favorite pastimes in the country. What do you suppose has changed?"

Gabriel reined his horse in, allowing the rest of the hunting party to continue on. Christian halted beside him. Ahead, Somersby lifted his shotgun and bagged his fifth grouse. Seabright only had one, and as a result, the betting between his friends had increased. "This house party was meant to provide a bit of sport and relaxation before the move back to Town. With Caroline's arrival, it has been anything but calming."

His friend slanted him a knowing look. "You have not found relaxation from the first night. I grant you that Caroline has not improved your mood, but she cannot be blamed for not getting what she is here for."

Damn the man for being more observant than most.

"I've seen you with dozens of women, Gabriel. I've never seen you as you are now."

"Nonsense."

Christian held up a finger. "You haven't enjoyed even half the entertainments you planned during this house party." Another finger went up. "You've been annoyed with friends you've known for years." A third finger. "Instead of joining the first hunt, which I know you anticipated, you agreed to teach Lily to dance. But after the first try, you pushed her into my arms, knowing full well that I hate to dance. Then you spent the rest of the afternoon glaring at me anytime my arm went around her."

"I admit that Lily has captured my attention. Holding her close that day made me want things best left private. I didn't trust myself with her."

"Mm. She's not your usual fare." Christian's blond locks fell over his forehead as he fished in his inner pocket for an object wrapped in his handkerchief. It appeared to be round, and gold. The man always had some mechanical project he tinkered with. "You prefer blonde, voluptuous widows who know what they are about." His cheeks heated. "Lily is voluptuous, I'll grant you, yet she doesn't exude the same elegance that you seem to prefer."

"If I told you to bugger off and leave this conversation alone, would you do it?" Gabriel asked.

Christian smirked. "Not for a moment. You dragged my arse here under threat of forcing me into my own carriage at gunpoint like a highwayman. It falls upon my honor to return the favor. It's what friends do."

Gabriel snorted. Christian and he had formed an unbreakable bond at Eton, fighting against older classmates who thought to bully those they considered weaker. Christian had been the first. At the age of thirteen, Gabriel stopped an older student from caning Christian near to death. He'd sent the senior to the hospital that day. They'd been the best of friends ever since. If anyone could understand Gabriel's plight, it was this man.

"Lily is different from the others. She's genuine. She isn't trying to trap me into marriage or worm her way into my affections so that I might shower her with jewels and pretty gowns."

"You did buy her a new wardrobe, did you not?"

"I did. I suspect the only reason that she accepted was because she had nothing of her own and didn't want to continue borrowing gowns from Violet." Gabriel thought back to their first kiss in the library and the sweet taste of her passion. "The more time that I spend with her, the more I find that I want to."

"Is it only her differences that make her compelling? A minor fascination?"

"No. It is also our similarities. She lost her parents when she was eighteen and had to raise a younger sister." Gabriel squinted at the party ahead. What the bloody hell was Seabright doing with his gun? Gesturing with it as he spoke?

"Gabriel, how did Lily come to be here with no belongings? I've heard her mention looking for a way to get home. It can't be so simple as hiring a coach, or I suspect she would have left a short time after arriving. Even passage to America can be arranged with relative ease."

He saw the unasked question in Christian's gaze. Lily wanted to go home but wasn't sure how. Christian was one of the most brilliant minds of their time. If anyone could help her, it was him. So why was Gabriel struggling to talk about it?

He wasn't completely certain that he believed in time travel. That didn't mean that it didn't exist, however. And he trusted Christian with all of his secrets. He knew he could trust the man with Lily's as well.

Christian turned his attention to the contraption in his hands while Gabriel struggled to find a response. He slotted a red flap over the gold piece, working it back and forth like a hinge. "As an aside, I don't think Seabright should be allowed to handle weapons. He gestures with them like his cigars."

Gabriel agreed. "It is quite possible that Lily is not from here."

"I gathered as much when she indicated she wanted to go home."

He met Christian's gaze. "Lily believes she is from the futu—"

A loud crack rent the air, followed by a woman's scream, and the whinny of a horse. Gabriel turned back to the rest of the hunting party in time to see Musgrave slide from his horse to land in a heap on the ground. The others froze.

Gabriel spurred his hunter forward. He heard the *thud-thud* of horse hooves behind him and knew Christian followed.

He reached his guests in less than a minute. Caroline's eyes were wide, covering her mouth with her gloved hand. Noah knelt next to Musgrave, pressing down on his shoulder. No one else moved.

He slid from the saddle and ran to Musgrave's side. The tinny smell of copper overpowered the crisp air. Blood was slowly turning Noah's handkerchief red. "What the hell happened?" he barked as he pushed Noah's hands aside and pulled Musgrave's jacket open. Birdshot had struck his shoulder and appeared lodged inside the man's body.

Hugh Musgrave moaned and jerked away from him.

Christian pressed another handkerchief to the wound. "Send someone for the doctor. We should be able to move him back to the estate with minor damage if we're careful."

Gabriel glared at the stiff, shocked people surrounding them. A shotgun lay on the ground. "Noah, ride for the manor and have a carriage sent for Doctor Wells at once." The man pushed to his feet and ran for his horse.

"Somersby—"

"It was me," Seabright interrupted. He visibly trembled as he tried to point to the gun on the ground. "I don't know what happened. It fired just as Musgrave said we should try to find one last grouse. He...he fell."

Gabriel stood and faced his longtime friend. "I think it best that you return to the manor with the others. Musgrave will live."

Seabright looked down at the weapon, then trudged to his horse. "He just fell. I don't know what happened."

"I'll get Hugh back to the house," Granville said. He turned to give Seabright a foot up into his saddle. The man's eyes were glazed, and he seemed confused.

"Somersby, please make sure that the guns are returned to my study." The man nodded, and soon the rest of his guests were riding away.

Gabriel knelt beside Musgrave. Christian had removed his cravat and wound it around the man's shoulder, holding the bloody handkerchief tightly in place.

"It will hold until Doctor Wells arrives," he said as he finished knotting the linen.

Hugh's eyes opened, lines of pain bracketing his mouth. "I feel like a bloody grouse."

"I fear Seabright's days of hunting are over," Gabriel said. "We'll get you to your feet, then you'll ride with me. The doctor has been sent for."

"Seabright needs spectacles if he can't tell the difference between a man and a bird," Musgrave grumbled.

Together, Gabriel and Christian helped Musgrave to stand. It would be a long, slow ride home.

THE CARRIAGE WAS parked in front of the druggist storefront, and a single footman waited by its door. Doctor Wells stepped out of the shop, followed by another man in livery, just as Violet reached them. "Doctor Wells, is something amiss?"

"Lady Violet." He removed his hat when he spotted Lily and Patience bustling up behind her and gave a short bow. "Ladies." He cleared his throat and tightened his hand on his black doctor bag. "I am called to Hawthorne. It seems someone was injured on the hunt today."

Violet paled. "Injured how?"

The doctor glanced at the footman, then back. "He was shot."

Lily's heart iced over in her chest, and her throat grew tight. *It can't be Gabriel.* She pressed a hand to her throat.

Violet latched on to the doctor's dark brown coat. "Who was injured?"

The older man shrugged and tugged his sleeve from her clutches. He adjusted his wire-rimmed spectacles and pushed his hat onto his head. "I'm not certain."

"Word is Lord Musgrave, my lady," one of the footmen said. "Lord Rothden and Lord Huntington were riding back wit' him while we fetched the doctor here."

All the breath rushed from Lily's lungs. She swayed under the force of the relief she felt. Gabriel was okay.

Patience grabbed Violet's hand when the younger woman paled. "Let's return quickly to see if we can be of assistance."

Violet's eyes were wide, and a tiny tremor wracked her frame.

Lily took her other side, and together, she and Patience walked

Violet back to their carriage. They rode back in silence. Patience cast worried glances at Violet who looked ashen.

"You don't think Gabriel shot him, do you?" Violet whispered as the carriage turned onto the drive.

"No," Patience said.

"What? Of course not, Violet." Lily took her hand. "Why on earth would Gabriel shoot his friend?"

"Because he pressed a flirtation with me?" Violet blinked, and moisture rimmed her eyes. She squeezed Lily's fingers hard.

"Violet, Gabriel loves you. He wants you to be happy."

"No, he doesn't. He wants me to be stuck here with him until I'm old and gray!"

Her words echoed many of the arguments Lily had with Bellamy. Bellamy felt stifled, and Lily had been too scared of losing anyone else to give her the space to grow into the woman she needed to be. She'd realized her error too late and ended up losing her sister after all. There was still some hope for her relationship with Bellamy if she got home. Just as there was hope for Violet and Gabriel.

The carriage rolled to a stop, and the door swung open. Violet took the footman's hand. The moment her feet touched the ground, she ran up the steps and disappeared into the house. Patience exited next.

As Lily alighted from the carriage, she looked up at the stone manor house, but her thoughts were on the family within. She owed them much for taking her in while she tried to figure out a way home. Maybe this was how she could repay their kindness. Lily was uniquely suited to help Gabriel and Violet with their turbulent relationship. She had already been down the road they traveled. She knew where it led. Maybe she could help them change course before it was too late.

She heard raised voices the moment she entered the hall and she followed the bellowing to the smaller anteroom next to the drawing room. Lord Musgrave lay on a sofa with his hands clenched and sweat dotting his brow. Christian knelt with him, holding him in place as Doctor Wells prodded the man's shoulder. Lord Seabright sat on a chair opposite with his head in his hands. Patience held her husband's hand as they stood near the window.

In the opposite corner of the room, Gabriel and Violet stood inches apart, yelling at one another.

"I did not shoot a man I've known for over a decade simply to turn you into a spinster, Violet. If that was my goal, I would forgo the blood and lock you in your room for a few years."

"Why allow me such comfort? Why not lock me in a tower...or...or a dungeon? Brick me up into a wall where no one will hear my cries. Then you'll be rid of me and my annoying need to have a husband and children before I'm dead."

Gabriel folded his arms over his chest. "You're acting like a child. I sent for Doctor Wells to see to Musgrave. His injury was an accident. Not an elaborate scheme to put you on the shelf."

"Just admit that you didn't like that he has an interest in me," Violet seethed. "You're happy that he's injured so now he won't dance with me at the masked ball."

Gabriel growled at her. "One more word of this nonsense, and you won't go to the ball."

Violet's eyes rounded, then narrowed. She poked him hard in the chest. "If you try to stop me, I'll elope to Gretna Green with the first man I see."

His jaw worked, and he clenched and unclenched his hands several times.

Lily sidled closer. "Violet, I think that Lord Musgrave could use another pillow. Would you get him one? Maybe offer him a bit of comfort when the doctor tries to remove the pellets?"

Violet stared hard at Gabriel several more seconds, then turned to Lily. "Of course. I'd be happy to offer Lord Musgrave *anything* he requires." She stomped away.

Gabriel snarled and made to follow her. Lily caught his arm. "Gabriel, I think—"

"Lord Rothden, might I have a word?" Doctor Wells adjusted his spectacles as he pushed to his feet and shuffled over.

Gabriel looked down at Lily, then took her hand in his and wound their fingers together.

Her heart warmed when she realized that he was seeking comfort through her touch.

"How may I be of assistance, doctor?"

"Removing the shot is quite painful. Normally I would advise that we give the patient laudanum for the pain."

Gabriel tensed, squeezing Lily's fingers painfully. *"No. Laudanum."*

She shivered at the dark command in his voice. He'd refused to give her laudanum when she'd awoken here with a concussion. At the time, she'd just been happy to not take an opiate. But the harshness in Gabriel's words, the glitter of anger and something else in his eyes, told her that there was something more here.

The doctor swallowed and nodded. "Then I advise a lot of liquor. And fast. I don't want him to lose much more blood."

Gabriel gave a single nod. A vein throbbed in his temple.

The doctor returned to his patient and asked someone to fetch him clean water and linen.

Lily stepped in front of Gabriel before he could follow. She put her hands on his chest. "Gabriel, are you okay?"

He stared over her head for a moment, then looked down. His eyes were far more green than gold, and small lines creased his forehead. "No," he whispered.

Lily took his hand and led him out of earshot of the others. "Is Lord Musgrave's wound very bad?"

"No."

That was good at least. "Doctor Wells seems capable. I'm certain Musgrave will be fine."

His lips thinned, but he rubbed his thumb over the back of her palm.

"This is more about what Violet said, isn't it?"

Gabriel lowered his head and pressed his forehead to hers. "In part," he said at last. "It is also the laudanum."

Lily wrapped her arms around his waist, sensing he needed the comfort. She didn't care that the others could see the small intimacy. "You can tell me anything."

His hands slid around to her lower back. "When my father died in that riding accident, I had to leave school to come back here and see to the estate. It was in far worse shape than I expected. My father had no head for business, and we were nearly to the point of selling off everything. I spent the first few months just stabilizing our accounts until we no longer bled money. I didn't realize that something else was wrong until Violet came to me crying because she'd rubbed the skin from her knee when she fell out of a tree. She should have gone to our mother for that sort of thing."

"Why didn't she?"

Gabriel glanced down at her. "She had. She couldn't wake my mother up. I called the doctor, only to be informed that my mother had refused to see him. She preferred to buy her laudanum directly from the chemist."

"What happened to her?" Lily was almost afraid to ask. Had the woman overdosed?

"She woke the following day, having no idea that she'd slept for a full day and night. She never inquired about Violet. Instead, she called for tea and pleaded being tired. It didn't take long to figure out that Vi had been taking care of herself while I was busy with the estates. Our mother chose not to deal with her feelings of grief. Instead, she wanted increasing amounts of laudanum."

"It's made from the poppy flower, right?"

Gabriel nodded.

"In my time, doctors have come to realize that medicines created from it can be very beneficial for managing pain. It is also highly addictive. People will lie, cheat, and steal for more because their bodies demand it of them."

Something passed through his gaze. "My mother cannot live without it. Nor does she want to try."

"Where is she now?"

"I sent her away to one of our smaller estates. I won't buy the laudanum for her. If she needs it, she must find a way to get it herself. That was eleven years ago. I took on the responsibility of raising Violet from that point on, and I increased our holdings and finances to far surpass anything the family's had in hundreds of years."

They had so much in common, especially with their families. It amazed Lily that she could find someone she shared so much with two hundred years in the past. "When my parents died and my older brother couldn't come back to help, I realized that I had to be the one to take care of Bellamy and myself. My parents had worked their whole lives, but never saved much. I had just enough money to cover the costs of their funerals. After that, I had to get a job so we could afford to eat. Archer sent money from his military pay every month or we would have lost everything to bankruptcy.

"Bellamy left for college the moment she could get away from me. Archer's money had to go toward Bellamy's tuition, which meant that I had to sell our family home and everything in it. I suddenly found myself without a place to live, without my parents, and without my siblings. That's when I realized what I did wrong."

Gabriel frowned and pulled her against his chest. "Lily, what could you have done wrong? Was there a way to save your family home?"

She shook her head. "I was so afraid of losing Bellamy. We'd lost our parents already and Archer was on top secret military missions. I lived in fear of getting a call in the middle of the night saying that he'd been killed in action. I clung too tightly to her, Gabriel. I refused to let her date or spend much time with her friends. I was too strict about who she spoke with and what she did. I was just so afraid and I became overbearing. We argued constantly. I remember telling her one day that I was trying to protect her because I loved her. She said, 'You don't love me, Lily. You love controlling me. I hate you.' I'll never forget that." Lily took a shuddering breath. "She left for college a week later. She wouldn't return my calls for weeks, and when she did, it was because she wanted money for something."

She curled her hands in Gabriel's coat lapels. "I'm telling you this because I see that you are going down the same path with Violet."

He started to shake his head, but she put her fingers over his lips.

"Think about what she said today. She thinks that you would shoot one of her suitors. That you would rather brick her up in the wall than let her have her own family. She thinks that you don't love her."

He stilled.

"It might be too late for Bellamy and me, but it's not for you and Violet. Gabriel, she needs you to loosen the reins a little and let her grow into the woman she is meant to be. If you don't, then you will lose her. She'll run off with a man you don't approve of, and you may never see her again."

"I love my sister," he rasped.

"I know. I love mine, too. Don't lose your relationship with Violet. You raised her to be a smart woman who can make good choices. Don't treat her as anything different."

Gabriel bent his head to rest his forehead against hers. Behind them, Lord Musgrave hiccupped, then moaned.

Lily giggled.

"I will think about what you have said. Perhaps if I choose the right husband for Violet, she will see that I love her and only want the best for her."

She blinked, then pulled back to look at him. "You plan to choose

Violet's husband? Are you going to give her a say in the choice?"

"Of course not. I know what's best for her."

"Oh dear. Gabriel, if your parents had chosen a wife for you without your consent or your input, would you have been happy to marry that woman and build a life with her?"

"Certainly."

"Would you be able to love the woman? What if they had chosen the dullest woman you've ever met? Or worse, what if they had chosen me?" She elbowed him gently with the joke.

He traced her jaw with his thumb. "A dull woman I probably couldn't have loved." He met her gaze. "Had they chosen you... I suspect it would be quite the opposite. A man could easily come to love you, Lily Bennett."

Gabriel lowered his head and pressed a soft kiss to her lips. Then he strode across the room to help his friend.

Musgrave gave him a cheerful greeting and offered Gabriel a sip from the empty bottle of cognac in his hand.

Lily pressed her fingers to her lips. His words shocked her to the core. She could easily come to love Gabriel Hawthorne, too.

CHAPTER ELEVEN

LILY WATCHED THE maid pin the last of her ringlets up. She sat in front of a mirror at the small dressing table in her bedchamber, hardly recognizing herself. Two of her new evening gowns had arrived from the modiste earlier in the day, and she'd chosen to wear the sapphire-blue dress to the musicale that Gabriel hosted. It came with matching slippers and white gloves.

Even if she didn't feel like she belonged in this time, at least she would look the part, thanks to Violet. She knew her friend would be wearing a similar, beautiful gown. As would Patience Cradock and Caroline Montrose.

Lily grimaced. The woman made her feel like an imposter. But dammit, it was hard trying to fit in to this time, while still searching for a way home. Lily had no idea what to do next, except to continue searching for something in the library that might help.

Images of kissing Gabriel in the shadowed room chose that moment to fill her thoughts. She clenched her thighs. God, the man could kiss. Every time she thought about the hot press of his body or the slide of his tongue, her nipples pebbled, and she got a little wet. Lily groaned. She would have dropped her head into her hands, but the maid chose that moment to tug a ringlet into place, pulling at her scalp. She cringed.

"Sorry, my lady."

"It's okay." The maid gave her an odd look but finished setting her hair. What was Regency-speak for "it's okay"? She'd have to ask Violet.

A soft knock at her chamber door broke her out of her thoughts. The door didn't immediately swing open, so it couldn't be Violet.

The maid sat her instruments of torture on the dressing table and opened the door to reveal Gabriel.

"May I come in, Miss Bennett?"

Part of Violet's instructions into social etiquette said that a gentleman was not to enter a lady's bedchamber. Lily had no intention of making him stand out in the hallway. *I'm not from this time, so I can plead ignorance.*

"Yes, of course," she said, standing up to greet him.

Gabriel stepped into her chamber wearing a midnight blue coat over an embroidered waistcoat and tan pants. His dark hair was swept off his forehead, and he was clean shaven.

She found herself a bit disappointed that the faint bit of five o'clock shadow was missing from his strong jawline. But then his eyes glittered down at her from his much taller height, and she forgot everything except the memory of his kisses.

The door clicked softly as the maid departed.

"You look beautiful," he said in that smokey voice that made her knees weak.

"Thank you." She smoothed her hands over the taffeta gown. "This is one of the dresses that Violet helped me pick out at the modiste." It was high-waisted, as was the current fashion, with embroidered vines and rosettes in matching blue thread across the bust, and along the hemline of the skirt. A tiny bit of ivory lace peeked out from the bottom of the puffed sleeves and along the top of the bodice. Enough to draw the eye if one were standing close.

Gabriel's eyes were drawn there now.

She watched him swallow, and a flush of heat seared her. She stepped closer.

His nostrils flared as he breathed deep, and his heated gaze met hers. "I shall have to send them my thanks," he rasped. "You are enchanting."

The room faded around them. Lily edged closer, placing her hands on his chest. "You're very handsome," she replied. His lower lip was a little fuller. She wanted to explore it. Did he feel this same smoldering attraction that she did?

He cupped her cheek in his big, warm palm. Feathered his thumb over her skin. "If I kiss you now, we shall miss the musicale." He didn't back away.

"That is probably supposed to be a deterrent."

"It is."

She leaned closer. "I'm not sure it's working."

He chuckled. "No." But then he took hold of her arms and put space between them. "I brought you a gift," he said.

"A gift?"

Gabriel smiled and reached into his coat pocket. He removed an item wrapped in a silk handkerchief. He trailed the fingers of his left hand down her arm to capture her hand, lifted it, and turned her palm up to press the wrapped object in it.

"What's this for?" she asked as she unwrapped the silk. Beneath was a jeweled comb. She gasped. "Are those sapphires?"

He smiled. "Indeed. When I heard you might wear a new gown of a similar color, I thought it would look beautiful in your hair."

Silver leaves twined across the top of the comb, accented by flowers with sapphire petals and small seed pearls. There had to be at least thirty cut sapphires. Her hand trembled. "I've never seen anything so beautiful."

Gabriel leaned down and whispered in her ear. "I have."

The smoldering look in his eyes made her breath catch.

"May I?" He plucked the comb from her hand, gently turned her back toward him, and nestled the comb into her pinned curls.

Lily had expected it to be heavy, but she barely felt its weight.

Gabriel cupped her shoulders and guided her over to the looking glass.

He stood so close behind her, that she felt the heat of his body. Lily looked in the mirror, first at the man standing behind her, then at herself. She blinked back a bit of moisture that filled her eyes. "I um...I've never worn anything like it. Thank you for letting me borrow it," she said.

He shook his head. "It is yours, Lily. A gift. My grandmother would have loved to see it on you."

"Your grandmother's? Gabriel, I can't keep—"

He spun her around and pressed a finger to her lips. "You can, and you will. She was very much like you. I think she would have loved you."

"She was a woman from the future who had no idea what she was doing?"

Gabriel chuckled. "Who knows. Annabelle Hawthorne was a woman of mystery, humor, and eccentric in her own way. It wouldn't surprise me in the least if she had traveled from the future."

"How long ago did she die?"

"Twenty years ago, perhaps. My grandfather loved her so dearly, that he soon followed. I think he couldn't be another day without her."

"Do you think love like that happens often?"

He shook his head. "If it did, great romances would be far more commonplace."

Lily smiled. "I'm glad they found love."

"I am, too. Shall we go down to the musicale? It promises to be dull, but it is what the guests want."

"A ringing endorsement. How could I say no?"

Gabriel grinned and held out his arm.

Lily gathered her shawl and gloves, and they went downstairs to the salon.

Gabriel escorted her to a seat beside his sister and Lady Patience.

"Ladies, please enjoy yourselves," he said. He gave Lily's hand a brief squeeze and then joined some of the other gentlemen by the sideboard. An array of drinks and light snacks had been set out, and people filled their plates.

"Have you been to a musicale, Lily?" Violet asked.

Patience looked startled. "Hasn't everyone?"

"I...don't think so," Lily said. "Not like this."

"These events give us an opportunity to gossip while listening to other people singing or playing musical instruments," Violet said.

"Not always well," Patience added under her breath.

Violet snickered. "It's not polite to plug one's ears, but if Lady Catteforde chooses to sing, I advise you do it anyway."

Lily bit back a smile. Her gaze wandered over to Gabriel. He stood with Christian and Zeph, listening as Lord Somersby spoke while spreading his hands to show the size of something. As if Gabriel could feel her regard, he turned his head and met her gaze. He gave her a slight nod, and the tiny smile that edged his lips made her heart beat faster.

"What instrument do you play, Lily?" Patience asked.

"I... don't know how to play any." Joining the high school band hadn't really appealed to her when she could spend her time in the library.

Patience's eyebrows rose. "Can you sing?"

Lily shook her head. Singing in the shower definitely did not count.

Violet patted her hand. "Neither do most of the people who will regale us with a song."

Lady Montrose walked by in a swish of dusty pink taffeta. She moved with an elegance Lily was quite familiar with. Head held high, shoulders back, and a bit of a sway to her hips.

Oh my God, she's just like Bellamy.

As Lily watched, she sauntered over to Gabriel's group and insert-ed herself into the conversation as if she belonged there. She took his arm and leaned into his tall form, looking as if she'd done it a hundred times.

Music began to fill the room as one of the men sat at the pianofor-te and played a spirited song. The guests took their seats, which finally managed to separate the woman from Gabriel's side. Lady Caroline Montrose, with her perfect smile and practiced laugh had taken all of two minutes at country dance to make Lily feel like a bug under someone's slipper.

She floated across the room as if too angelic to tread on the carpet, nodding and smiling as she passed people.

All hail the queen, Lily thought as something dark twisted her in-sides. She closed her eyes long enough to stomp on the negative feelings. The woman was probably perfectly nice in her perfect way. Perfect for Gabriel. Lily may have been blessed with his passionate kisses in the dark of night, but she knew better than anyone that it meant nothing. She had no claim to him. Besides, she was going home as soon as she figured out how.

The next hour passed in a jumbled mix of delightful music, horrid solos, and pleasant choruses. Lily did her best to enjoy each entertain-er. Patience played the harp for a beautiful song, and Violet played the pianoforte in a dramatic piece that seemed every bit as wild as she.

Gabriel asked who would play next, when a sultry voice behind Lily spoke up.

"Miss Bennett, won't you play something from the colonies for us? I would love to hear what music is popular there," Lady Montrose said.

Lily paled as all eyes turned to her. "I... I'm afraid that I don't play, Lady Montrose."

"How about a song then? You must have the most beautiful singing voice."

Something in the woman's tone had Lily turning in her seat. Caroline's smug smile said she knew Lily would refuse.

She's intentionally trying to embarrass me. Again. She must have overheard Lily tell Violet that she couldn't play or sing. Dammit, it was working. Her face and neck felt hot.

"I'm certain you would outshine me," Lily replied in a low voice.

Caroline smiled in triumph. "As am I." Then lower so that only Lily could hear, she said, "You don't sing, you don't play an instrument, you don't dance...what *do* you do, Miss Bennett? Aside from go after men well above your station?" When she rose from her seat, she said to the small gathering, "I fear our Miss Bennett is too shy. I shall play in her place."

Violet took Lily's hand. "I'm sorry," she mouthed.

Lily nodded, sinking a little lower in her chair.

Caroline sat at the pianoforte as if she'd been born to it and sang a song about lovers reuniting.

Nearly all eyes were glued to the woman who commanded the room. All but Zeph, who looked Lily's way. She ducked her head, afraid she might see pity there. After the song concluded, loud applause erupted. Even Gabriel clapped.

Of course, he clapped. He's the host, Lily. And even if he wasn't, the song was beautiful. Lily gave a half-hearted clap of her own.

Lord Twisden called for an encore, and several others echoed. Lady Montrose smiled, met Lily's gaze for a split second, and then began to play another song.

Gabriel smiled at his ex-mistress and settled back in his seat to enjoy her performance.

God, just when she felt a little more comfortable in this time, Bellamy's Regency twin had to show up to remind her of what she would never be. Graceful, beautiful, sophisticated...she was still just a woman without a home and a family that barely talked to her. A woman that a gorgeous, powerful man like Gabriel would never really want. Not when he could have Bellamy. Er...Caroline.

"Lily?" Violet whispered.

She turned to find a watery version of Violet's concerned face. Shit, she was about to cry. *No.* Hell no. She wouldn't give Caroline the satisfaction.

"It's been a long day, I should lie down." The words rushed out of her, but Lily didn't care. She mustered every ounce of dignity she had and left the room.

》》》×《《《

PETTY MEANNESS WAS not an attractive trait in a woman. How had he missed it when he pursued a relationship with Caroline? Gabriel narrowed his eyes and his lips thinned as she played her second song. Her little mischief with Lily moments ago had not gone unnoticed. He'd almost stepped in to save Lily any embarrassment when Caroline announced that she would play.

Once, he had thought her one of the most beautiful women in all of England. Now, he knew her coy looks were carefully fabricated, and the need for praise was what truly lay beneath the lovely facade. Vanity could turn a person into a cruel viper.

"I wonder what that's about," Christian murmured from the chair beside him. He'd been fiddling with the face of a clock for much of the musicale.

Gabriel followed his friend's gaze to see Lily slip out the door. "Perhaps she's off to the retiring room?"

Christian snorted. "If that were the case, wouldn't she have at least one other woman in tow? Isn't there a law that says they must freshen up together?"

Noah Cradock sat forward from the row behind them. "If it is, I

136

say we address it in Parliament this session so that I might spend more time with my wife."

The pull Gabriel felt to go after Lily, to keep her in sight, startled him. He needed her nearby. He drummed his fingers on his thigh. What if she was upset by Caroline's mischief?

A movement caught the corner of his eye. Across the narrow aisle between rows, Violet surreptitiously waved to gain his attention. She opened her eyes wide and then nodded toward the door Lily departed through. Blast. Vi wanted him to go after Lily.

He stood as Caroline played the final notes of her song. His guests applauded, and Twisden called for another. Gabriel waved the man off.

"Friends, the hour grows late. Let us enjoy supper. If you'll join me in the dining room?" He waved his guests toward the door, keeping his gaze locked on Caroline.

She basked in the glow of the praise for her music and slowly made her way toward him. "I sang the first song for us, darling. Did you enjoy it?"

Gabriel grasped her upper arm and towed her to a corner of the room. "I do not appreciate your attempts to embarrass one of my guests, Caroline."

She rolled her eyes. "The mousy Miss Bennett? How was I to know that she didn't sing or play?"

It was unlikely that Caroline would know, and yet… "All the same, I saw the look you gave her when you sat at the pianoforte."

"I simply wanted to show her how ladies of good breeding are raised. Although she isn't a lady, is she Gabriel? She is only *Miss* Bennett of America." She smiled silkily.

"Whether she is a milkmaid or the queen of England, it is no concern of yours, Caroline. You will be polite to my guests, no matter their station."

"Darling, I don't know why you're acting this way." She put a hand on his chest and leaned closer. "If you must know, I wanted to make clear to her that a wallflower like herself would never capture the interest of an earl. I was trying to help her. Getting one's hopes up could lead to a broken heart in a woman such as she." She shrugged. "Is that so terrible?"

He ground his teeth, biting back a retort. Lily might be a wallflower, but she smelled sweet. Unlike the rose that stood before him, withering with every word that left her mouth. He grasped her wrist and lifted it away from his body. "How very altruistic of you."

She narrowed her eyes.

"Whether Miss Bennett captures my eye or not is also no concern of yours. As you may recall, I ended my arrangement with you at the end of the Season. I will tell you once more. You will be polite to my guests, *all* of my guests, while you visit this house. If I find that I need remind you again, it will come with the insistence that you return yourself to London at once. Have I made myself clear?"

Caroline pulled her wrist out of his grip. "Quite. Clear."

"Very well. Then do enjoy supper, Lady Montrose. I understand my cook has made an excellent meal for the evening." He spun on his heels and stalked from the room.

Gabriel took the stairs two at a time. Lily's bedroom door was open. He hesitated only a moment, then entered. Lily stood in front of the fireplace with her arms crossed over her waist, staring at the flames. Her shoulders were tight. He could feel the tension rolling off of her.

He stepped into the room and closed the door behind him. "Lily."

When she didn't turn, he crossed the distance between them and wrapped his arms around her from behind. Her body was tense, nearly vibrating against him. He pressed his cheek to the top of her head. "I'm sorry about Caroline."

She pulled out of his arms and spun to face him. Her hands balled. "You're *sorry*? How many times will she try to embarrass me? You know what? Don't answer that. I've taken care of myself since I was eighteen. I won't let that woman get to me any longer. So what if I can't sing or dance or paint or have men falling at my feet? I don't need any of that." She took a step away from him. "And I don't need anyone who believes I do."

He cocked his head. "You think I care if you're accomplished in what Society thinks a lady should know? I don't give a whit about any of that, Lily. I never have."

Her chin lifted. "I saw you smile when she started her second song. You heard her goading me down there, and you smiled at her after. You still love her."

Gabriel moved toward her, crowding her until her back hit the wall next to the fireplace. He put his palms on either side of her, caging her in. "I never loved Caroline Montrose," he seethed. "She's selfish, vain, and sometimes cruel. Do you honestly think that is the kind of woman that I would love?"

She pressed her lips together and looked down. "No."

"I did not smile at Caroline. I was furious with her for her antics both tonight and at the dance."

"It didn't look like it."

Gabriel put a finger under her chin and tilted her head up to meet his. "If she even looks at you wrong, I will throw her out of this house that very minute. Reputations be damned."

She frowned. "What about making a good match for Violet?"

"My sister would rather I send Caroline away on the first coach than see you upset. Violet really cares for you, Lily." He traced his thumb over the line of her jaw, losing himself a little in her eyes. When he spoke again, his voice sounded rougher. "I care for you also." He placed his other palm over her heart. "It angered me to know that Caroline aimed her daggers at this sweet heart."

"I think the reason it bothers me so much is because it drags up old memories of my fights with Bellamy. In many ways, Caroline is a lot like my sister. They're both tall, blonde, and beautiful. They both have ways of getting what they want. As a teen, Bellamy knew just where to strike to hurt the most during our arguments. Caroline does the same." Lily hesitantly placed her hand over his on her heart. "She believes she still has a claim to you. Does she?"

Gabriel shook his head. "I grew tired of her company to the point that not even our time abed was pleasurable. She never had my heart, Lily."

She reached out to press her hands against his chest. "What does it take to win Gabriel Hawthorne's heart?"

The air thickened between them as she met his gaze. "No one ever has." But if anyone could, he thought, it might just be Lily.

She tugged her lip between her teeth, then rose on her toes to kiss him.

The kiss turned from sweet to passionate in the space of a heart-beat. Gabriel dragged her against his chest and slanted his mouth over hers. She melted into him, stroking her tongue against his. Every touch incinerated his control. He wanted to pull her back into his lap to touch her the way he had the other night. To taste her. He wanted her naked underneath him. Gabriel dragged his mouth away, pressing his forehead to hers.

"Every time we kiss, I want more," he said roughly.

Her hands went to his cravat and pulled the knot free. "I want you, too, Gabriel."

He caught one of her hands in his. "Lily, if I touch you, I may not have the willpower to stop myself from taking you to my bed."

She studied him in the dim candlelight, and he saw understanding flash in her eyes. Good. She knew that he meant to respect her propriety in this.

"I'm not a virgin, Gabriel. I… I know I'm not very good in bed, but I want to be with you. If you want me, that is."

His breath stalled, and his heart kicked against his chest. She wanted him to take her. He stumbled on her other confession. Someone told this woman that she wasn't good in bed? He didn't want to think of her naked in the arms of another, but he couldn't let the comment pass. "It takes two people to create passion, Lily. If you showed even an ounce of the fire you show me, then any problems in the union of bodies were not your failing."

She pressed a soft kiss to his lips. "I don't know how much time I have here, Gabriel. But I know that I want this."

It took less than a heartbeat to make a decision. He swept her into his arms and turned toward the bed. The canopy with the green coverlet lay several feet away. He could have her under his hands in seconds. He changed direction and strode toward the door panel separating their rooms. One touch and the door swung open. He strode through and deposited her on the heavy velvet coverlet of his bed.

Gabriel had never had a woman in this bed. Whenever a woman had spent time here at Hawthorne, he'd taken them in the chamber that Lily currently occupied. This was his sanctuary, and he'd never wanted another in it. But having Lily anywhere else felt wrong. She belonged here, amid his crisp white linens and bed curtains.

Gabriel yanked off his cravat and closed the panel between their rooms.

Lily had kicked off her slippers and was trying to pull the delicate jeweled comb from her hair when he returned to her side.

"Allow me," he said. He worked the comb loose from her hair and set it on his bedside table. Then he speared his fingers into her hair, pulling free those silky waves. Hairpins clattered to the floor all around them.

Lily grinned and worked the buttons of his waistcoat open, then spread her hands across his linen shirt over his abdomen.

He divested himself of his coat and waistcoat, then spun her around to unlace her. Their fingers bumped as she tried to help, and she let out a throaty chuckle that went straight to his cock. Good Christ, he was hard for her already, and he hadn't even seen that smooth skin yet. In moments, her dress and petticoat pooled at her feet, followed by her stays.

Gabriel turned her in his arms, wanting to see every inch of skin revealed as he pulled her chemise over her head. "You're a goddess," he breathed.

Lily's full breasts were tipped with pink nipples, already hardening under his gaze. Her skin felt silky beneath his hands as he ran them up her bare arms and down her sides to the flare of her hips. She had more curve to her hips than many of the women he'd been with, and he found he quite liked them. He traced the curves with his hands and followed them to the rounded globes of her bottom. Between her thighs, she had a strip of golden-brown hair. Not the triangle of curls he expected.

Lily fluttered a hand over her mound. "Women often wax themselves down there."

"Why?"

"Um. A lot of reasons. The desire to be seen as pretty there instead of...furry?" She flushed pink. "And uh, sometimes it's more comfortable when you live in a hot climate."

Gabriel traced the strip of hair with the backs of his fingers and hummed. Then he removed her garters and set her back on the bed. He unrolled each of her silken stockings, tracing the skin he revealed with his mouth. At the arch of her foot, he lightly bit her, making her gasp.

Then her hands were on him, shoving at his linen shirt. "I want to see you. Take it off."

He slipped the braces off of his shoulders, then made quick work of the buttons at his throat. He pulled the shirt over his head and heard her quick intake of breath.

"God, you're gorgeous." Lily sat up and pressed a kiss to his bare chest. She ran her hands over the muscles of his chest and across his shoulders, then over each ridge of his abdomen. "I didn't expect you to have such muscle definition."

"What did you... *Ahh*." Gabriel hissed when her fingers stroked over the front flap of his trousers, molding to his shaft.

She opened the buttons and reached inside to wrap her hand around his cock.

He groaned as he captured her hand in his. Any more and he would spill right there.

Lily licked her lips as he kicked his shoes off and removed the rest of his clothing.

The sight of her tongue stroking along her lips, leaving them damp, drove him mad. Gabriel cupped the back of her head and pulled her mouth to his in a fierce kiss. Their tongues stroked together.

He broke the kiss only long enough to pull the bed linens down. Lifting her in his arms, he settled her in the center of the bed and crawled over her. The feel of her warm skin flush against his body made the breath rush from his lungs. The next breath he took was fully Lily. Roses and female. He settled between her thighs. She was hot and wet against him. Like heaven in his arms.

Lily hooked her legs over his, pulling him closer. They kissed until they were breathless. He trailed hot kisses down her throat and between her breasts. He savored their weight in his hands and sucked one nipple into his mouth. She undulated against him, quiet little moans falling from her lips as she buried her hands in his hair.

Gabriel switched to her other breast, lavishing attention on it while he stroked and squeezed the other. He wanted to spend hours learning her body. Finding every small place that made her moan and those that made her scream in pleasure. This first time, he knew he wouldn't be able to wait. He needed her.

He slid a hand between her thighs to stroke at her wet folds. She lifted her hips, asking without words for what she wanted. Gabriel moved lower, shouldering his way between her thighs. He breathed in the spice of her arousal.

She shivered when he exhaled over her skin. "Yes," she whispered, gripping his hair harder.

He needed no further invitation. He'd dreamed about this moment. Leaning forward, he licked her and groaned at the taste of her. "Delicious."

Lily's back arched with his next lick.

He sucked and savored, licked and laved her until she trembled beneath his mouth. Only then did he push a finger inside her.

"More," she cried.

Gabriel pushed a second finger in, then found the hard nub that begged for his attention. He sucked it, flicking his tongue over it, and pumped his fingers.

"I'm… I'm going to…" Lily bucked beneath him as she came.

He licked her through her orgasm, bringing her back down slowly. She panted beneath him, trembling after her release.

"Oh my God, Gabriel." She reached for him, trying to pull him up her body. "I need you."

He rose over her and settled his hard cock against her heat. Warm, wet folds enveloped him, and it was all he could do not to shove inside her.

Lily wrapped a hand around his cock and stroked him, then lined him up with her entrance. "Don't make me wait," she said. She licked his lower lip, then kissed him hard.

He met her kiss, drinking deep from her as he pushed slowly inside.

"I love tasting myself on your lips," she said against his mouth.

He grunted, unable to speak as her tight heat gripped him. Not even Caroline had wanted his kiss after he pleasured her. That Lily loved that sexy, forbidden flavor made him want her all the more. He pushed hard, filling her to the hilt.

They both groaned.

Gabriel pulled back an inch and thrust. Lily sighed and wrapped her legs around his hips, holding him close. He began to move then, thrusting harder, then faster. His blood pounded in his ears, and he watched her face for signs of what she liked. He angled his hips, and she cried out his name. Gabriel slammed into her, rocking them both into the mattress. He skimmed a hand between their bodies and rubbed at that nub until she arched against him, scraping her nails down his back. The sensation speared him, and he came with a harsh growl.

When he could think again, he lowered himself to her side and pulled her into his arms.

Lily sucked in steady gulps of air, one hand trailing over his arm.

He buried his nose in her hair near her neck, letting her scent wash over him. Whoever had told Lily that she wasn't good in bed with a man was an imbecile. She'd come alive for him as no other woman ever had.

Her hand stilled on his arm. "It's never been that good," she said quietly.

Gabriel rose over her again and captured her lips in a tender kiss. "Never," he agreed.

She looked up at him with wide eyes. "You don't have to say that."

He tucked a damp strand of hair behind her ear. "Then I shall have to prove that I mean what I say."

Whatever she saw in his gaze seemed to assure her. She snuggled into his embrace.

He rolled onto his back and pulled her to his chest. Sleep tugged at him. As he succumbed to tiredness, he heard her soft words.

"That's the sweetest thing a man has ever said to me, Gabriel Hawthorne. I hope you mean it."

In his heart, he knew that he did.

Chapter Twelve

THE MUTED CLINK of metal on metal pulled Gabriel from sleep. He heard the thunk of wood hitting the fireplace grate and saw the flare of flames between the slim opening in his bed curtains. The maid had come to stoke the fire, warming the room from the chill that had set in overnight.

He looked down at the woman asleep in his arms. He'd made love to Lily again in the middle of the night, then pulled the curtains closed before tucking her into bed beside him. He should have sent her back to her chamber for propriety's sake. But hang it all, he hadn't wanted to let her go. He knew the servants would talk belowstairs but couldn't bring himself to care.

The moment he heard the soft thump of the door closing behind the maid, he stroked his hand over Lily's side from her shoulder down to her rounded hips. He loved her body. Loved the way it fit against his as he thrust between her thighs. Loved her very full breasts and the soft plane of her stomach.

She murmured something and nestled back against him, rubbing her arse against his growing cockstand.

His hips bucked, seeking her heat.

Lily's eyes fluttered open, and she yawned, then looked over her shoulder with a sleepy smile. "You weren't a dream."

"Do I feel like one?" he asked as he palmed her breast and gently rolled her nipple.

She arched into his touch, which rubbed her plump bottom against his length. "Mmm, no. You feel wonderful."

Gabriel chuckled and pressed a kiss to her neck.

Lily rolled him onto his back and straddled his hips. Her hair fell in tousled waves around her shoulders. Thank God it wasn't long enough to cover those beautiful breasts. He'd barely been able to tear his gaze away when they were bound in the snug bodice of a dress. Now that they were free and within reach, he was enraptured. He'd loved breasts since he'd been in school and discovered the wonder of a woman's body. But Lily's fit just right in his hand. He squeezed her gently and thumbed her nipples, then rose up to suck one into his mouth.

She rolled her hips against his and held him to her. "That feels so good," she said.

Gabriel wrapped an arm around her waist and urged her to lift. She raised onto her knees, and he positioned her over his cock.

"But I wanted to taste you," she said.

"Next time. I need you." He urged her to sink down onto him.

Lily let out a sigh when she'd taken him fully.

Gabriel pressed his forehead to hers, waiting for her to adjust. He'd never felt anything so good in his life. Bedding a woman had never felt like this. Like finding the place his body belonged.

He opened his eyes and met the liquid blue green of her eyes in the dim light of the fire seeping through the bed curtains. He didn't want Lily to leave. The realization froze him in place. He didn't want her to find a way home, because to him, she was home. Right here in his arms.

She wiggled against him. "Move, Gabriel. I need you."

Her breathy words reached into his heart, tugging at him. *I need you.* He wanted her to say those words again but in a different context. He wanted her to need him in her life, not just her bed. The feeling sent a sliver of fear through him.

"Gabriel?"

"Ride me." He gripped one hip to help her move and curled the other hand around her shoulder, pulling her down with every thrust up. With her body clutching his, he could focus on this feeling, here, now.

She found a steady rhythm, hips grinding against him. Her breath sawed in and out of her lungs, gusting against his temple as he worked her body hard.

This was faster, harder, needier than their earlier joinings, which had also been intense. He licked his thumb and reached between them. He pressed on her nub, rubbing it in a circle. Lily cried out as her orgasm took her.

He pumped his hips when she lost the rhythm, and when her body stopped clenching on him, he rolled her onto her hands and knees and thrust into her from behind.

Lily screamed into the soft ticking and gripped the linen sheets. She pushed back against him and fell into another wave of pleasure. The walls of her body pulsed around him, dragging him over the edge with her. Gabriel leaned over her, barely keeping his weight off as he poured his seed into her.

Lily sagged onto her stomach, breathing heavily.

He rolled off of her and tugged her into his arms.

A moment later, she went stiff and sat up. "Gabriel, you came inside me."

"Several times."

"I'm not on birth control."

He stilled. He'd never once forgotten. Not even as a lad with his first woman. He ran a hand over his face. "If there is a babe, I'll take care of you both."

"What if I find a way home and then find out that I'm pregnant?" she whispered.

"Then I shall have to find a way to follow you," he said simply. There was no way he would leave Lily to raise their child alone. If he had to fight the strands of time for her, then he would find a way to do so.

She scrambled away from him and knelt on the bed. "You can't mean that."

He sat up. "Why wouldn't I?"

She waved her hand around. "You can't give up all of this to follow me, Gabriel. I don't have a house. I barely have a job." She paled. "I can barely support myself. How could I ever support a baby?"

He reached for her and she flinched. He paused, then grabbed her upper arm and tugged her back to his chest. "Lily, there is no guarantee that you will carry our babe. If you do, then I will be with you."

"I can't let you give up your life, your title, for that."

"You also can't stop me from doing so."

She searched his gaze for long moments. Then she threw her arms around him and held him tight. "I really like you, Gabriel Hawthorne."

He chuckled and pressed a soft kiss to her temple. "After spending the night in my bed, I certainly hope so."

She reared back and pushed his shoulders until he fell back onto the mattress. She straddled his hips and cupped his cheeks.

When she didn't say anything more, Gabriel pulled her mouth down to his. Just before he kissed her, he murmured, "I like you, too, Lily Bennett."

⋙⋘

AN ALMOST TANGIBLE excitement filled the air as the final preparations were made for the masquerade ball. Dinner and cards in the drawing room last night had been filled with tales of past masquerades and anticipation of tonight's ball. Throughout the day, the staff of Hawthorne had carted loads of fresh candles, decorative silks, and decorative feathers into the ballroom. Neither Lily nor Violet had been allowed a peek at the decorations. Reginald stood guard at the doors like a lion, snarling at anyone who tried to sneak in.

Violet was currently plotting to steal out the back and try to see the ballroom from the veranda. She'd come to Lily's chamber to get ready for the ball.

"It's not fair that Gabriel is keeping this a secret. I was the one who wanted the ball. He wouldn't have had it at all if not for that." Violet laid her gown out on Lily's bed. She'd chosen a light pink shepherdess dress with a white lace mask.

"Perhaps he wanted to do something that would make this night special for you," Lily said. She sat at the dressing table while a maid finished pinning up her hair. Though Violet and Gabriel had found a truce after their argument a few days ago, Lily knew that Violet still harbored some anger. It came through at odd moments, like now.

"For you, maybe," Violet mumbled.

"Finished, my lady," the maid said. She'd curled Lily's hair into pretty ringlets with gold ribbon.

"Thank you. We will ring if we need anything else," Lily replied.

The moment the maid departed, Lily went to her friend. "Gabriel loves you dearly. That's why he's been a bit overbearing." She held her hand up to ward off Violet's protest. "He told me about your mother and the laudanum addiction. It happened not long after you lost your father, right?"

"Yes. Father died when I was eight. Mum went to live at one of our estates right after I turned nine. Gabriel doesn't like to talk about her." Violet tilted her head. "Why?"

"It must have seemed as if you lost both your mother and your father."

"It did. I didn't understand why Gabriel was so angry with Mum that he would send her away when she was sick. It wasn't until the next time I visited her several years later that I realized that he did it to

THE EARL'S TIMELY WALLFLOWER

take care of me because Mum couldn't."

"Gabriel lost them both also, Violet. He was called home from school to claim his title unexpectedly, found the estate in jeopardy, his mother drugging herself, and no one to care for you. When my parents died, and I was left to care for my younger sister and keep us from losing our home, I was terrified that I would fail. I thought I'd lose her, too, so I clung too tight. I acted like Gabriel sometimes does."

"You said you hoped to repair your relationship with your sister. What happened?"

"She felt as you did. That I didn't love her and didn't want her to be happy. She left for college and didn't speak to me for months." Lily looked down at her hands. "I lost her. The very thing I was trying to avoid. But I do love her, and I do want her happiness. I just didn't know how to give her what she needed and not fear that the moment she had it, she'd run away and I'd never see her again."

Understanding dawned in her eyes. "That's why he hasn't approved any of my suitors," Violet said. "I threatened to elope with a stranger to Gretna Green."

Lily bit back a laugh. "Maybe instead of doing something that drastic, you could talk to Gabriel. Try to understand his fears. It's what I wish had happened with Bellamy."

Violet nodded, then hugged her. "I wish you could fix what happened with your sister, Lily, but I'm afraid it's not possible."

Her brows drew together. "Why not?"

"Because I won't allow you to leave us. Your sister will just have to come here."

She laughed. "I don't think that's how it works with time travel."

"How do you know? Have you found a way to return?"

"No."

"Then you *have to* stay. Gabriel needs you."

"But I—"

"He's different with you. I know he cares about you. Don't you care for him?"

Lily swallowed. "I do. I—I'm conflicted. Part of me says I don't belong here, and another says that I've never felt more at home. I never thought I'd make such good friends two hundred years in the past."

Violet shrugged. "I hadn't expected a sister-in-law from the future, but the more I think about it, fate probably had to look that far in advance just to find someone who would suit my brother."

Sister-in-law? The thought of being married to Gabriel sent warmth curling low in her belly. That was a dream she could want so easily. If only there weren't so many barriers in the way. Lily forced a small laugh. "I'm not sure I'm what the Earl of Rothden needs."

"You're what *Gabriel* needs. What we both need. Don't go, Lily. Please."

CHAPTER THIRTEEN

L ILY HAD NEVER felt more beautiful than she did descending the stairs of Hawthorne Hall to attend Gabriel's masquerade. The gold silk gown hugged her bodice and hips, then draped in soft folds to the floor and ended in a small train. Gold lace gave the illusion of off the shoulder sleeves and cupped the underside of her breasts. Feathers painted gold and sewn onto two panels hung down her back. The final touch was a half mask decorated with more, tiny feathers and pearls. She'd been uncertain about the idea when Violet suggested it to the modiste, but when she'd put on the costume this evening, she couldn't fault her friend's choice.

Violet waited for her on the landing, looking adorable in her costume. "Hurry! Most of the guests have arrived."

Lily laughed, feeling the same sense of anticipation. There was a magic in the air. Many of the candles had been doused, leaving large patches of shadows in the hall. The soft strains of music poured from the ballroom, mixing with the laughter and conversation of the many guests. The dining room was open with an enormous spread of food, and several guests mingled there over cups of punch.

Two footmen in domino masks stood at the entrance to the ballroom, looking more like part of the decorations than real men.

Violet pulled Lily past them, and they had their first glimpse of the ballroom. Hundreds of candles glowed in the crystal chandeliers high above the dance floor. Thick ribbons wrapped around the columns, and swaths of black, red, and white silk created little alcoves along the edges of the room, beckoning couples to steal a few kisses.

"It's perfect," Violet breathed.

Lily hadn't expected there to be so many people. The country dance from earlier in the week seemed empty by comparison. She spun slowly, admiring the many costumes. With the shadows and the masks, it was hard to recognize anyone. Would she even recognize Gabriel?

Someone bumped into Lily's arm. She turned to see a tall man in a black velvet tailcoat and red brocade waistcoat. Diamonds winked on his snowy cravat, tied in a complicated knot, and a red satin ribbon fob. Behind the simple domino mask were stormy blue eyes and disheveled blond hair. He smelled faintly of oil.

"Christian?"

"I fear you've found me out, dear Lily."

"I almost didn't recognize you with your straight cravat," she teased.

Mirth glittered in his eyes. "Reginald insisted on tying it. Seems I cannot be counted on to do so properly. He insinuated that a perfect knot was part of my disguise."

She pressed her lips together to contain her laugh.

"May I say you are beautiful as a golden bird. A perfect pairing."

"Thank you. Pairing for what?"

His lips quirked. "Perhaps you will grant me a dance later? After Gabriel, of course."

"I would, but I know you hate to dance."

"For you, I would make an exception."

Her heart softened. Christian had no desire to be here, yet he not only attended, but stepped outside his comfort zone to make those he considered friends happy. Any woman would be lucky to have him, and she fervently hoped that a very special woman found him soon. "I would love to."

"Then I shall hunt for you later." He gave a short bow and melted into the crowd.

When Lily looked around, Violet was gone. She edged her way through the masses. There were magicians and knights, fairies and pirates, queens and Turks. Noah and Patience were dressed as a Roman emperor and empress, and she spotted them talking to a man dressed as a sailor and gesturing with his cigar. It must be Lord Seabright.

Where was Gabriel?

Dancers twirled on the dance floor to a minuet, and a woman cackled nearby. Wandering amid the costumed crowd, with the string music, and shadows gathering along the edges, it felt as if she'd entered another world.

A subtle, woodsy scent caught her nose. Lily turned, seeking the source. There. The faint scent of pine and musk teased her senses. It was a fragrance that she'd know anywhere. *Gabriel.* She followed, rising on her tiptoes, trying to catch sight of him. Then the crowd parted just enough to reveal the profile of a tall, strong man wearing a brown and gold mask. Her heart pounded.

He turned, and their eyes locked. Sound faded, the shadows cleared, and only Gabriel remained. He wore a dark green tunic under a leather jerkin and leather breeches. Bracers covered his forearms, and thin leather straps dangled from around his wrists.

A slight smile touched his lips. "I knew I'd find you, my golden lady hawk," he said in a husky voice. "My sweet bird always returns to her master."

A perfect pairing, as Christian had said. The bird and the falconer.

He took her hand and drew her to him. Lily pressed a hand over his heart, feeling the heavy beat. "She knows where she feels safe," she said.

Gabriel grazed her temple with his lips. "There's nowhere else I'd rather she be."

The air between them thickened, and heat flooded her lower belly. She wanted to draw him into one of the alcoves and make love to him again.

"Dance with me, love."

She nodded. He took her hand and led her to the dance floor. The musicians played a waltz, and he took her in his arms. Gabriel expertly guided her around the floor. Lily, lost in the moment, didn't worry about tripping or stepping on his feet. One song bled into another, and then another.

Violet once told her that it was scandalous for an unmarried woman to dance more than two songs with the same man in a row, but Lily didn't care. At the end of their fourth dance, the musicians began a lively reel, and Gabriel led her off the dance floor and into the shadows. Partygoers flowed around them, laughing and drinking. With her hand in his, they moved easily through the crowd. He paused at the edge of the room, scanned the surrounding people, then twirled her into an alcove.

Red and black panels of silk muffled the masquerade beyond, enclosing them in their own, private world. Gabriel pulled Lily into his arms and lowered his mouth to hers. He kissed her with the same hunger she felt burning inside. Deep and heady.

Lily opened her mouth to him, savoring the decadent flavor of brandy on his tongue. She speared her fingers into his hair at the back of his neck and held him closer, needing the contact.

Gabriel leaned back against the wall, spread his legs wider, and pulled her between them.

She felt the hard outline of his cock and moaned softly. She wanted this. Needed Gabriel like she'd never needed another.

He moved, tugging at his wrist while he kissed down her neck. "Do you trust me?" he breathed in her ear.

Lost in sensation, Lily nodded.

His dark chuckle was the only warning she had before he captured her wrists and pulled them behind her back. Something wrapped around her wrists, binding them there. Lily tugged and realized that it was the leather strips from his costume. The falcon master had caught her.

"Now that I have you, my little bird, what shall I do with you?"

The husky seduction of his words made her wet, and she clenched her thighs. "Anything," she whispered. "I'm yours, master."

His eyes flared in the dim light. Then his hands were delving under her skirt, sliding up her thighs. "No petticoat," he murmured just before his fingers slid through her folds.

Lily moaned against his neck. Pleasure swamped her, and it was all she could do to keep quiet.

Gabriel took her mouth in a consuming kiss. He wrapped one arm around her waist, holding her tight to his chest as his other fingers played her body, winding her tighter.

Someone could enter at any moment.

The thought that someone might discover them, made Lily both nervous and hotter. Her core clamped down on the two fingers thrusting inside her. She buried her head against his chest. Gabriel flicked his thumb over her nub, back and forth, thrumming her. Faster and harder. She trembled, muscles locking. It had never felt so good. Her body wept, and she let out a low moan as she came.

He kissed her softly, bringing her back down.

Lily sucked in gulps of air until she could breathe steadily.

"If I could, I would take you right here," he murmured. "I fear that would not only ruin our costumes, but that I wouldn't be able to part from you until well into tomorrow." He straightened her dress. "I will never forget this moment."

There was a tenderness she'd never seen before in his face or any other man's. "Neither will I."

"Stay with me?"

Lily looked deep into his hazel eyes. Did he mean tonight in his bed? Or longer? Would he ask her to stay in this time with him? Is that what she wanted?

He dropped his gaze. "I want to make love to you again, Lily. Say you'll stay with me tonight."

"Yes. I'll stay."

He smiled, but it didn't quite reach his eyes.

Did he feel as disappointed as she did in that moment? It was as if they were both reaching for more but dare not say the words.

His fingers stroked the inside of her wrists, then the leather straps released.

Lily rubbed her wrists absently.

Gabriel cupped her cheek and pressed a kiss to her lips. "Until later, love." Then he slipped out of the alcove.

Her feelings were a jumbled mess inside her heart. She had a job and family waiting for her to return, but her heart wanted her to stay. If she didn't find a way home, it was likely a moot point anyway. But what if one day, years from now, something accidentally zapped her home? She couldn't bear to think of loving Gabriel only to lose him unexpectedly. She had no idea what to do.

Lily peeked around the silk curtains and saw that the people around her were looking at the dance floor. She slipped out of the alcove unseen and moved away. Caroline, dressed as a Greek goddess, danced with a highwayman. It was easy to make out the woman's perfect waves over one bare shoulder and the confidence with which she held herself.

"They dance well together, but are an odd pair," Christian said as he stepped up beside her. "I don't think Zeph particularly likes the lady."

She tried to hold back her chuckle and failed. "I think the high-wayman costume suits him."

His lips quirked. "Will you grant me that dance now?"

She agreed, and they danced a merry quadrille. Lily was laughing when he escorted her off of the dance floor. A servant came up to them in his dark suit and domino mask. He held out a note.

"Your pardon, my lady. The lady requested that I deliver this."

Lily thanked him and opened the note. It was from Violet, requesting that Lily come at once to the library. She needed to talk urgently.

"Have you seen Violet?" she asked Christian.

"No, is something amiss?"

"Probably not. She wants to talk to me. I shall find her."

He nodded, raised her hand to his lips in a brief kiss, and thanked her for the dance. When he left, Lily thought she saw his shoulders relax as he headed for the ballroom doors. She suspected he might be returning to his room now that his duty as a friend was concluded. Somehow that endeared him to her a little more.

Lily scanned the crowd but didn't see Violet anywhere. Gabriel was most likely engaged with his guests. She left the ballroom and went up the stairs to the library. The door was cracked, and the glow of candlelight spilled out into the hallway.

"Violet?" she called softly as she pushed the door open and stepped into the room.

Instead of a sweet shepherdess, a Grecian goddess stood in front of the fire, wrapped around the muscled body of a falconer.

Gabriel held Lady Montrose in his arms, kissing her.

Lily's heartbeat pounded in her ears, and a chill swept through her body, settling in her chest. Another image formed over the top of their forms. Her ex-boyfriend Mason, pressing a redhead against the wall with her legs wrapped around his hips, after a show. He hadn't invited Lily to the concert. She'd never met his band members in the four months they dated. She bought the ticket, intending to surprise him. Instead, the surprise was on her. Just like it was now.

Lily spun to leave and bounced off of the doorframe. She didn't look back. Didn't want to see Gabriel kissing another woman. When would she learn? How many times had she told herself that an earl would never pick someone like her? Gorgeous men liked gorgeous women. It was a law of nature.

Gabriel may not have wanted to turn her into Bellamy, but in the end, he'd wanted a woman just like her sister.

She ran back down the stairs and skidded to a halt in the middle of the entry hall. She turned, looking for a way out, when a pink shepherdess stormed out of the ballroom. A man with a sling on his arm hobbled after her.

"Come near me again, and I'll have my brother shoot you the next time," Violet hissed at him. Neither seemed aware of her.

With a start, Lily realized two things. One, Violet looked ready to smash Lord Musgrave in the head with a shepherd's crook. Two, she hadn't sent the note asking Lily to the library.

Caroline. Lily glared up the stairs as if she could see the woman from there. She'd sent the note specifically so that Lily would catch them kissing. Her hands clenched, and a burst of fury made her flash hot. She was done with Caroline and her jealous attempts to get Gabriel back. Lily wasn't normally one for violence, but she was going to march back into the library, yank Caroline off Gabriel by her perfect blonde hair and slap her perfect face.

She halted three steps up the flight of stairs. Her shoulders slumped.

Did it matter if Caroline kissed Gabriel? Yes, he wanted Lily now. But what about a month from now? A year? What if she found a way to go home? All the thoughts and fears from earlier crowded her head, spinning round like a mad group of dancers, until her head began to throb.

She stood frozen on the step until movement caught her eye. Zeph descended, looking every bit the dashing highwayman with his black coat and long cape. A black quarter mask cut diagonally across his face, making him look dangerous. He stopped beside her on the step and tucked something into his pocket.

A necklace?

"You look lost, Miss Bennett."

She *was* lost. In so many ways.

Zeph reached for her hand and wound it through his arm. "Let's take in some air, shall we? When I feel lost, sometimes getting lost further will put me back on course."

What odd comments he makes. The man is an enigma, Lily thought as he led her through the ballroom and out the veranda doors into the garden beyond. Chilly night air cooled her flushed cheeks and released more of the anger from her body.

They wandered down a bricked path lined with flowers fighting the onset of winter. A sliver of silver moon cast little light and she was grateful for the torches spread every few feet.

"Have you ever found yourself at a crossroad and didn't know which way to go?" she blurted. The maelstrom of emotions still churned up her insides.

"Often. Some of my own creation even." One side of his mouth curved up in a mischievous grin. He reminded her a bit of the Cheshire Cat from *Alice in Wonderland.*

Lily couldn't help but smile back. The heavy feeling in her chest lifted a little. "How did you decide which path to take?"

"I made my own path down the center, of course. But that is what *I* would do. You want to know what *you* should do." He stopped to smell a flower. When he looked at her, the light caught his silver-gray eyes, giving them an almost ethereal glow.

"No matter which path I choose, I lose someone I care about."

"Love should play a big part in any decision, should it not?"

Did she love Gabriel? Her heart clenched. "I suppose it should," she said softly.

Zeph nodded and started walking again. "One thing to remember, Lily. The future isn't written yet. Not even yours."

She looked up at him sharply.

He stared straight ahead, a slight smile teasing his lips. "And if you truly cannot decide which path to take, make your own down the middle."

Lily couldn't help it. She laughed.

They walked for several more minutes. "May I return you to the hall, Miss Bennett? I have a few items to return to some of the guests."

"Like the necklace in your pocket?"

His teeth flashed white in the darkness. "What fun is there in playing a highwayman without the full experience? Never fear. I shall return all of their valuables."

"Just don't rob any coaches tonight," she teased.

"I make no promises."

⟫⟫⟫⟪⟪⟪

THE THUMP OF something nearby wrested Gabriel out of Caroline's surprise kiss. She'd asked him to the library, then thrown herself into his arms like an eager puppy. He pushed her back a pace. A flash of gold pulled his attention toward the noise. A single feather twirled as it floated to the floor.

Blast! *Lily.*

He spun to find Caroline smiling with her arms crossed. "What have you done?"

"I've missed you, Gabriel. I know you miss the passion between us."

"You purposely orchestrated this little incident. You sent me that note to meet you here, just so that Lily would catch you kissing me, is that it?"

Caroline lifted a slim, bare shoulder. Every aspect of her Grecian goddess costume was meant to entice a man. "I don't know why she would come here. Let's not talk about her, darling. I gave you these last months to rejuvenate out here, though I can't comprehend what you find so endearing about the country. Nevertheless, you'll be returning to London for the Season soon. Come back to me, darling. Let me love you the way only I can."

How had he ever found this woman attractive? Was she so insecure that she would set up this little scene to drive a wedge between he and Lily? He wanted his little wallflower to stay, and Caroline just gave her a very large reason to leave. Heat flared in his veins, burning through him. He clenched his fists. "I knew you were jealous, Caroline, but I had no idea you would stoop to cruelty to try to get your way. What a fool I was to ever seduce you," he bit out.

She sucked in a breath.

Gabriel crowded her until her knees hit the back of a chaise, and she sat. He leaned over her. "You will return to your room, you will pack your trunk, and you will leave my house immediately."

"Gabriel. Please, I—"

"If I ever hear from you again, I will ruin you until you dare not show your face in Town. Have I made myself explicitly clear in this, Caroline?"

"*Gabriel.*"

"Get. Out." He kicked a chair out of the way and stormed to the door. "A carriage will be waiting to take you into the village the moment you are packed," he called over his shoulder. "I'll send a man up to make certain that is within the hour."

He stalked from the room to find Lily. He took the stairs two at a time up to her room. The chamber was empty. Where would she have gone? She'd become friends with Violet. Perhaps she'd sought his sister out. He spun and rushed down the stairs.

Violet stomped up them with a clenched jaw and red cheeks.

Gabriel hadn't seen her this angry in some time. He stopped her and took hold of her shoulders. "What is it, Vi?" Had she already heard of Caroline's schemes?

She drew herself up to her full height and said with all the authority of the prince regent, "Next time you go hunting with Lord Musgrave, you have my permission to shoot him again."

"I didn't shoot him the first time, Violet. I suspect a magistrate would not accept my explanation that you gave your approval, were I to put a second wound in his arm. Why this urge for violence against the man? I thought you—" he swallowed around the sudden lump in his throat—"I thought you liked him."

"That was before he tried to coax me into the garden for a kiss. When I refused, he tried to steal one anyway."

"*What?*" he growled.

"I was so angry that I stomped on his foot," she seethed.

A muscle ticked in his jaw. "Good. I'll—"

"Then I elbowed him."

"—deal with him—"

"*And* slapped him." She crossed her arms over her chest and hunched her shoulders. "I might have overreacted."

If Gabriel wasn't so furious, he would have laughed at her confession. Before he could throw his former friend out, though, he needed to take care of both of his women, starting with Violet. He wrapped his arms around her and pulled her into a hug. "I'm proud of you, Vi," he said.

She blinked up at him. "You are?"

"You didn't let some young buck ruin you, even though you thought you might like him. I should say though, that you missed your chance for Gretna Green."

She hugged him back. "I'll find someone else to elope with if I must."

"You won't." Lily was right. Violet had grown into a smart young woman. In part, because he'd raised her to be so. But he couldn't take all the credit. His Vi was a force all on her own. Tonight, she'd shown him that he could loosen the tight hold he had on her. Maybe, if he helped Violet find the right suitor, she wouldn't leave him. Maybe she would want to stay close by and share her new family with him. "When the Season begins, I'll do what I can to find you a suitable husband."

She poked him in the chest. "Not just suitable, Gabriel. I want to love him the way you love Lily."

He stilled. Then his heart began to pound. Did he love Lily? Just the thought of losing her because of Caroline's antics had sent him into a rage. He couldn't lose her. Not to Caroline and not to time. Good Christ. He was in love with Lily Bennett.

"I like her, Gabriel. She makes you happy."

"She does," he admitted. "But Caroline has caused mischief again. Lily may not want to stay."

"Then you must convince her. She's yours. Ours. Part of our family now. I don't want to lose anyone else. Please, Gabriel."

He looked down into Violet's big eyes. "I don't want to lose anyone either, Vi. Especially not Lily."

He had to find her, *show* her that he wanted nothing more to do with Caroline Montrose. Lily had appeared as if by magic in his life. Though she was nothing like what he thought he wanted, she was everything he needed. Fate entwined their paths. Gabriel would follow her through the strands of time to keep her.

CHAPTER FOURTEEN

*T*HE FUTURE ISN'T *written yet. Not even yours.*

Zeph's words played on a loop in Lily's head as she returned to her room. She had no desire to go back to the masquerade ball. There were too many things to sort through in her heart.

Make your own down the middle.

That last one seemed impossible. How could she make a path down the middle of either going home to her century or staying here? Ending up in 1917 didn't seem like it would solve anything. God, she was so mixed up.

She dropped her head back and stared at the ceiling as she shuffled down the hall towards her room.

A thump and a masculine curse sounded as she passed Christian's chamber.

Lily stopped at the open door and peered inside. The man was on all fours under a desk. He crawled back and sat on his haunches, rubbing the back of his head. One of his shirt sleeves was rolled up while the other was still cuffed, and part of his shirt had come untucked from his pants. She spotted his coat and waistcoat half hanging off of the bed.

"Christian, are you all right?"

He scowled but nodded. "Dropped the last piece under the desk." He held up a curved piece of something about two inches high. It had an unusual red sheen with gold filigree.

Lily's gaze snagged on it. She drew closer.

He sat on the chair and picked up a tool, then hunched over the desk and fit the piece into something else.

Propriety said Lily shouldn't be in his room alone, but that particular red was like a siren in her memory. She couldn't look away.

"There," he said, and she heard the smile in his voice. "At last. This one has been months in the making."

"What is it?" she asked. But she knew. Her heart skipped a beat, then began to slam out a fast rhythm.

Christian swiveled in his seat and held up a red enamel egg with pretty gold filigree. "It's a clock. It opens here, and when the hands strike the hour, these two dancers come together and spin in a... Lily? You've gone quite pale."

She met his gaze. "Holy shit. *You're* the clockmaker." All this time she'd been searching for either the clock or any indication of who might make something so beautiful and advanced, only to find out that she'd been under the same roof as the clock this entire time. Somewhere out there, the Fates were laughing their asses off.

Bitches.

"Ah... It's actually called an automaton, which is actually just a self-operating mechanism that controls another aspect of the piece, making it move independently of the other parts. You see, the dancers are powered by the movement of the clock, which, when properly fitted to the..." He flushed. "Apologies. Sometimes I forget myself and speak above most people's understanding."

"I've seen a few other automata, but they were much larger and either steam or weight operated. Nothing so small and intricate. Or quite so powerful."

His eyes closed for the briefest second. "You have no idea what a pleasure it is to speak with you, Lily. Gabriel is very fortunate."

She must have made a small sound because he gave her a concerned look. "I love when the dancers come together and the gentle-man raises his hand to take the lady's."

"How could you know that? No one has seen it work."

Her throat went tight. "It brought me here." And it could take her home. The elation she thought she'd feel when she found the clock never came. Instead, she felt like an elephant had settled on her chest. She couldn't draw a full breath.

Christian rubbed his thumb over the little hinged door. "It brought you here from the future," he said.

Her eyebrows shot up. "How did you know?"

"Gabriel started to say something during the hunt. He was inter-rupted, but I worked out the rest. Are you certain it was *this* clock?"

"Have you made more than one?"

"No. This one took months. Even if I chose to make another, it wouldn't be exact. I would probably choose a different part to move when the hands mark the hour." He squinted at the piece. "It should operate like a normal clock. I don't see how... What I mean is, it *is* a clock. It records the measure of time. It shouldn't control the flow of it. Is that something that people have harnessed in your century? Can anyone travel in time? Can they choose where they want to go? Is it only the past or is it possible to go forward into the future? Is this the first trip for you?"

Lily reached out to touch the clock, paused, then stroked a finger over the enamel. "No. Most people think time travel is impossible. There have been scientists to hypothesize the probability and people who've tried to create devices. But as far as I know, no one has been successful." But then, she had been, hadn't she? Who would ever know about it if she stayed?

Was she staying?

Christian studied her a moment. He took her hand and turned her palm up, then gently set the clock in her hand.

It was a little heavier than she remembered. The doors were open, and the clock read half past three. The little gears inside ticked as they turned.

"I haven't set the correct time on it," he said.

"I set the hands to midnight when I had it at home."

"Perhaps that is the magic hour?" He covered her hand with his. "What will you do, Lily?"

"I don't know."

"Gabriel cares a great deal for you."

"I care about him, too."

Christian released her. "I am pleased to have met you, Lily Bennett. I hope we have many years of friendship ahead."

She smiled but knew it didn't reach her eyes.

He waved her off. "I must clean up. Then I have to sketch a few new ideas."

Lily closed her hand gently around the little enamel egg and held it to her chest. "Thank you, Christian."

"If you leave, that is likely the last I will hear those words. My dearest friend will never utter them."

She pressed a kiss to his cheek, then rushed from the room. The clock was in her hands. She could go home. But did she want to?

THE CLOCK CHIMED two in the morning when Gabriel climbed the stairs again. He hadn't found Lily among the guests. Unfortunately, he'd been waylaid several times as host of his own damn ball. The last of the party goers were filing out of the ballroom, stifling yawns and removing their masks.

He rubbed the knuckles on his right hand. Despite her earlier incident with Musgrave, Violet had recovered her disposition in her usual rapid manner and enjoyed herself. Gabriel smiled. The sole reason he'd held the ball was to make her happy. Before meeting Lily, he had not looked forward to the event. Filling his house with many of the same people he wished to avoid during his respite seemed like madness.

Ah, but when he'd seen Lily in her delicate costume, he'd been grateful to his sister for the idea. And those stolen moments in the alcove? Magical.

He hoped Lily wouldn't be asleep yet. There were things he need-ed to say.

Gabriel climbed to the second floor and walked down the hall towards his chamber. Lily's door was open once more, and bright light blazed from within. He stopped on the threshold, admiring the curve of her hips in her lovely dress as she stood in front of the window. She looked lost in thought as she watched the line of carriages slowly depart.

"Lily."

She dipped her head, then slowly faced him. "Gabriel."

The distance between them felt far greater than the few feet that separated their bodies. He crossed to her, watching her face carefully. Was she angry about the kiss she'd witnessed in the library? Hurt that he would kiss his ex-lover so shortly after bringing her to a climax? He couldn't read her expression.

"I didn't kiss Caroline. Not willingly at least. She threw herself at me the moment she heard you entering the library. It was all a scheme to push you away so she could capture my affections again."

"I know."

He stopped in front of her. Lily's face didn't betray any emotion, and that in itself worried him. She often wore her heart on her sleeve. The Lily he knew was genuine even in her hurt or embarrassment. The woman before him had stuffed her emotions far away. Gabriel hated the change.

"There is nothing between Caroline and I, and there never will be. Even had I not met you, I wouldn't want her. But I did meet you. Lily, you've changed everything for me."

"I'm sorry about that," she whispered, looking down at her hands.

"What? Don't be. I would have lost Violet if it weren't for you. She would have eloped and never spoken to me again. You made me see that I was pushing her away with my actions. When I offered this house party, it was because I wanted a bit of respite before my duties began anew. Despite all the activities I looked forward to and the company of my friends, none of them gave me the peace I sought. *You* did."

Her forehead wrinkled, and she finally met his gaze again. "Gabriel, I..." She lifted her hand up. Cradled in her palm was a little, red enamel egg with gold filigree.

He frowned. "Is that the contraption Christian has been working on this last week whenever he could escape an activity?"

She nodded.

"Why do you have it? Did he gift it to you?"

"It's what brought me here."

"What?" Gabriel had to swallow twice to wet his suddenly dry throat. Every muscle in his body went tight.

"This is the clock that brought me here. Christian is the clockmaker I searched for."

"How is that possible? The damn thing's been in pieces all week."

"He was building it. He...he didn't even know what it did. But somehow, he created a device that cuts a hole in time and allows people to move between centuries."

"You have the means to go home now." Why now? On the very night that Lily was subjected to Caroline's machinations? When her heart would hurt from seeing a scene much like the one that ended her last relationship? Would fate truly be so cruel as to give him the woman he wanted above all others, only to rip her away again?

She closed her hand around the clock and held it to her chest. "I do."

"Will you use it?"

She looked up, and he saw the storm of confusion and uncertainty in her eyes.

Gabriel's heart jolted. There was still time. He could convince her to stay with him.

"I don't know," she whispered. Her voice hitched on the last word. "This entire time, I told myself that if I found the clock, that I would go home and fix the relationship with my siblings. Find out if I could purchase the cabin and make a true home for us. I told myself that I didn't truly belong here."

"You do belong here, my love. Look at how you've become a part of our lives. Violet adores you. I have never seen Christian say more than a dozen words to a woman, yet he seems to enjoy speaking with you. There's an ease about him that I've never seen before." He couldn't hold back any longer. He had to touch her. Gabriel closed the remaining distance between them and cupped her cheek. "As for me, I have loved every moment of your company. Even when I thought you might be mad and in need of a physician's care."

She choked on a laugh.

"You belong with me, Lily Bennett."

She covered one of his hands with hers and closed her eyes. "I don't know what to do."

"It's okay to want things for yourself, love."

She blinked up at him. "I do. I want things."

His Lily had a beautiful, warm heart that wanted things to make others happy. He suspected that she didn't know how to do the same for herself. "The cabin you told me you wish to purchase. Is it for you because you love it? Or because you believe your siblings will love it?"

"I... It's nice."

Much as he thought. "The women of your time work, yes?"

She nodded.

"Did you enjoy your work? Are you returning for employment

that you love and don't wish to give up?"

"N-no. I mean, it was okay. I liked working for Mr. Samuel. It should have been my dream job, you know? But for some reason, I didn't like it as much as I thought I would."

"What do you dream of doing instead?" He felt like an arse for pushing her. Lily looked miserable, and it cracked his heart open to be the one causing her pain. But he needed her to see this for herself before she made a decision. Before she broke both of their hearts and he could never get her back.

"I don't know, Gabriel. Is that what you want to hear?" She pushed out of his embrace and wrapped her arms around her waist.

"There is nothing wrong in wanting things for yourself, Lily. To take hold of the things that make you happy. It's okay to want this. To want *us*."

"Gabriel, don't make this harder."

He switched tactics. "If you could have anything in the world, what would it be?"

She hunched her shoulders and ground out, "I don't *know*."

"There is nothing you dreamed of having or doing one day?" he pressed.

"No," she hissed. "After my parents died, I gave everything I had and then some to Bellamy. I worked until I fell asleep on my feet just to keep us in a house. There wasn't time to dream, Gabriel."

"After she left to study?"

"I didn't know what to do with myself. I sold everything we owned and split the money between the three of us. It felt as if we all went separate directions. Like I was lost in the woods, not knowing which way would lead me out, and knowing that no one would come looking for me. I had to make my own way because Bellamy and Archer were too busy with their own lives. I spent so long putting my dreams aside that I didn't know how to have them anymore. I thought... I thought that if I could bring us all back together that it would fix everything. It *will* fix everything. Once that is settled, then I can figure myself out."

She was leaving him. Gabriel could barely breathe through the ache in his chest.

Lily bit her bottom lip, then said, "I don't know what I want. I need time to figure it out."

"Then you must not want me as much as I want you." He hadn't meant to say the words. Hadn't realized they were even on his tongue until they were past his lips.

She sucked in a breath.

"If you did, you would know," he added, damning himself.

"It's not that easy."

"Isn't it?"

"No. How can it be? No matter which path I choose, I lose people that I care about."

"I would give up everything. For you."

"What?" She whispered the question as if she was afraid he would say the words again.

Gabriel held her gaze, needing her to see into his heart. "If the choice is living with you or with all of this—" he waved to the room around him—"then the choice is simple."

"You would give up being an earl? Having money to do whatever you wish? You'd give up your relationship with *Violet*?"

"Yes," he said without hesitation. He trusted that Violet would make her own way should he disappear tomorrow. His sister was bright and knew how to get exactly what she wanted in life. She would do well.

Lily's mouth dropped open at his response. "Why? How can you say that? How can you know that you won't change your mind in a month? Or a year?"

"Because I love you, Lily."

She froze.

Long moments passed as they stared at one another. When he realized that she wouldn't respond, pain stabbed him in the chest. He laid his heart at her feet and she couldn't even muster a response. She didn't feel as he did. She was leaving.

Gabriel took one step back. Another. When he reached the door, he nodded at the clock still clutched in her hand. "When you leave, at least do me the courtesy of saying goodbye."

Then he strode from the room and quietly closed the door behind him.

Violet stood in the hall, her eyes wide.

"You should say your goodbyes while you can," he told her.

Tears filled her eyes. "Gabriel…"

"Goodnight, Violet." He entered his bedchamber, closed the door, and turned the key in the lock. His body felt weighted down. Every movement an effort that he didn't have the desire to give. Gabriel removed his costume and climbed into bed. He hadn't changed into his sleepshirt, but it didn't matter. He didn't feel the cold. He didn't feel anything at all.

CHAPTER FIFTEEN

"**G**OD'S BLOOD. YOU look like hell, Rothden," Granville said as Gabriel shuffled into the breakfast room a few hours later. "Did you sleep at all?"

"No. A strong cup of coffee would not be amiss this morning," he replied. He pulled out the closest chair and slumped into it. "If this is the way you pay compliments, it is little wonder that the debutantes avoid you."

He hadn't slept at all during the long hours of the night. Instead, he replayed his last conversation with Lily over and over in his head, wondering if he could have said anything different to change her mind. If he could have done anything to make her love him the way he loved her.

Granville grinned. "I know precisely how to pay compliments to the ladies. I save the insults for my friends, as any good gentleman should."

Twisden, Seabright, and Somersby chuckled from their seats at the table. A buffet of scones and jam, and eggs and kippers, was laid out on the sideboard, and it seemed his friends had availed themselves to half of it.

A servant set a cup of coffee before him. Gabriel nodded his thanks and took a gulp of the bitter brew. His hand twinged, but he ignored it.

"I say, have you seen Musgrave this morning?" Somersby asked.

Seabright shook his head. "The Cradocks left early this morning. I suspect Albury is holed up in his chamber, inventing a way to motorize horses."

"Musgrave left overnight," Gabriel growled. He took another sip of coffee.

Somersby was watching him. "That have anything to do with why your knuckles are red?"

"Saw him before he left. His looks may improve once his nose heals," Twisden said.

Several pairs of eyes swung toward Gabriel. He sipped his coffee. Had Lily left? He'd asked her to say goodbye, but would she do so after their words last night?

"Musgrave pressed his suit with Lady Violet after she turned him down," Zeph said in his throaty voice as he strode into the breakfast room. He swept a pale strand of hair back from his face and plucked an apple from the fruit basket on the table.

Somersby scowled. "Surprised he's still walking. The imbecile."

"A few more minutes with the young lady and he may not have. She made her displeasure quite clear, and he has the bruises to show for it. I daresay the broken nose he received from Gabriel hurts less than his pride." Zeph pulled out a chair and folded his tall frame into it.

Speaking of Violet, she should have joined them for breakfast this morning. He set his coffee cup in its saucer. Damn. She was probably feeling as heartbroken as he was, knowing that Lily's departure was imminent. He would check on her after he saw the last of his friends off. The men gathered for breakfast were leaving today as the house party concluded. Only Christian planned to stay a few extra days.

The discussion around him changed topics to the news of Napoleon's moves in Germany.

Sometime later, Christian strolled in. He stopped when he saw

Gabriel. Then he moved to the sideboard to fill a plate.

The room went silent.

Gabriel blew out a breath. He knew this man as well as he would know a brother. Christian's movements were stilted, his shoulders stiff. "It's not your fault," Gabriel told him.

Christian didn't turn around. "If I hadn't built the clock..."

"If you hadn't, she wouldn't be here now. I would never have met Miss Bennett."

Christian looked over his shoulder. "Has she...?"

He rubbed a hand over his face. "Probably." When he looked up, four other pairs of eyes studied him. The only one not looking at him was Zeph. His pale friend took another bite of his apple as if the odd conversation was of no interest. "My sister's friend, Miss Bennett, is leaving eminently. Nothing to concern yourselves with."

Their reactions varied from confusion to suspicion. Blessedly, no one responded.

Soon, they were saying their farewells and making plans for visits to White's and Vauxhall Gardens in the coming weeks. Gabriel walked them out to their carriages and saw them off. Christian stood at his side on the front steps.

"What will you do?" his friend asked.

"I have work to attend to before we depart for London." He could go over every detail of the estate accounts for the last two years. That should occupy him for a few days. Maybe then he wouldn't think about the future. About Lily. "You need not stay. I've taken you away from your workshop for far too long. We shall see each other soon."

Christian slanted a look at him. Then he turned and stalked into the house.

Gabriel sighed and followed once the carriages were out of sight. When he didn't see Christian, he climbed the stairs to check on Violet. At the top, he glanced down the hallway. Lily's door was closed.

Was she in there?

He turned away from it and knocked on Violet's door instead. He heard her soft footfalls seconds before the door opened. Her dark ringlets were unbound and loose about her shoulders. She wore a simple, white morning gown, and he spotted her bare toes beneath the lace hem. "You weren't at breakfast, Vi. Are you well?" *Is your heart breaking like mine?*

"I didn't want to face that odious Lord Musgrave," she admitted.

"You shan't have to. He left overnight."

"Oh. I thought he was leaving today." She fiddled with a bit of lace on her sleeve.

"I gave him reason to leave early."

Her lips curled at the corners, and she looked at him from under her lashes. "You are a dear brother. Thank you for always looking out for me. And for agreeing to help choose the right suitor." Her smile fell. "Are you well, Gabriel?"

"Should I not be?"

She rolled her eyes. "If the love of my life was leaving forever, I daresay I would be a disheveled mess. Not looking as you do every day." She waved her hand to encompass his coat and trousers. "Although you are a bit paler."

"Lily made her choice. There is nothing more to say." He pressed a kiss to her temple. "If you need me, I shall be in my study."

Gabriel turned away. He didn't look at Lily's door before he descended the stairs again. He locked the pain in his chest away and went to tackle the accounts. The livelihoods of the people living on his estates depended solely upon him. He couldn't give in to the pain.

I WOULD GIVE up everything. For you.

Gabriel had uttered those devastating words to her. Professed his love, and she'd remained silent.

I'm such an idiot.

The first light of dawn had broken the horizon hours ago, and the sun now shone gaily through the bedroom window. Lily sat on the stool in front of the dressing table, staring at the clock that brought her here. She'd placed it on a pillow from the chaise lounge to keep it from rolling about and breaking.

After her conversation with Gabriel last night, she hadn't attempted to set the time and go home. She'd been up all night, searching her soul for the right decision. Her heart pointed one direction and her head the other. If she left, she might be able to restore her relationships with Bellamy and Archer. But there was no guarantee. She hadn't been very successful up to this point. Plus, she might not be able to buy the cabin. And even if she did, what reason would they have to leave their lives to stay with her? Bellamy had an apartment on Park Avenue in Manhattan. There was no way she would move to a tiny town in Kentucky to a cabin in need of updates just to be with Lily. God, Archer wouldn't even return her calls. Was there any way to even change their relationship?

If she left, she *would* lose Gabriel forever.

If she stayed, she would lose Archer and Bells, but possibly gain Gabriel and Violet as her family. Of course, there was no guarantee of that either. He might tire of her. Or meet another woman who was far more beautiful than she would ever be.

Lily rubbed her eyes. It felt like there was sandpaper under her eyelids. She and Gabriel also hadn't been careful when they made love. What if she accidentally wound up pregnant and went home? He'd never know he was a father and she'd have to decide if she was going to raise a baby alone.

Her head throbbed.

Way to go, Lily. Your life wasn't screwed up enough, so you went all out.

She looked back down at the clock.

Love should play a big part in any decision, should it not? Zeph had asked it as a rhetorical question when they walked in the garden last night.

Lily's heart had answered anyway: *Yes.*

The trouble? She loved them all. Especially Gabriel Hawthorne.

Her heart flipped over.

I love him. Do I really think that I can live without him?

No, and she didn't want to try. Gabriel was willing to give up everything for her. He would even try to come with her if she wanted him to. What if he couldn't though? What if the clock only worked for one person? She couldn't risk it.

She caught her gaze in the mirror. Hope shone there, mingled with a touch of excitement. Bellamy and Archer had their own lives. They would probably miss her. They might even worry, but they would go on without her. They had for years.

Gabriel was right. She'd been afraid to want anything for herself. Until now.

Lily wanted Gabriel. Now that she had the clock in her hand, had the option to use it, she knew that she wouldn't.

She picked up the clock and left the room. Christian answered his door on the second rap of her knuckles. He had a smudge of something on one cheek. The sight made her smile.

"Lily?"

She took his hand, turned his palm up as he had done to her the evening before, and placed the clock in his hand.

A silent understanding passed between them.

"It is selfish of me, but I am very glad that you will stay. I should have hated to lose another friend. I have so few, you see." Christian tucked the egg into his pocket.

"I would have missed you terribly as well. Now I don't have to."

"He's in his study, trying to bury himself in numbers."

She thanked him and hurried down the stairs to the floor below.

Reginald adjusted a bust that sat on a plinth in an alcove. He whipped his handkerchief out of his pocket and dusted the marble.

When he spotted her, he nodded his head, then left the hallway.

The study door was closed, but the knob turned under her hand. Lily pushed the door open.

"Reginald, for the love of God. Please go find someone else to bother," Gabriel muttered. His head was bent over a ledger of some sort, and he was crossing out lines with a quill.

"He's stepped away," she said.

Gabriel stood so fast that his chair tipped over and clattered to the ground. "Lily." At first, he seemed eager to see her. Before she could utter a word, the pleasure drained from his face, replaced with dread. "You've come to say goodbye then?" He bent to right his chair and sat.

Lily crossed the room. She hesitated, then rounded the desk to stand beside him.

He looked up when she laid her hand on his shoulder.

Lily gently pushed him back in his chair, hiked up her skirts, and straddled his lap.

He grabbed her hips to hold her still, and his brows scrunched.

"Gabriel Hawthorne, Earl of Rothden, Baron of Hawthorne, I love you. I know what I want now. I want you."

His eyes closed. When he opened them, she saw burgeoning hope. "I love you, Lily. I'll go wherever, whenever you go."

She shook her head. "I gave the clock back to Christian. I'm staying here. I don't want to risk losing you, and I don't know if you'd be able to travel with me. Besides, you made me see that it was time that I wanted something for myself. And there is nothing more that I want in the entire world except you, Gabriel."

His smile spread slow across his lips. Gabriel slid his hand into her hair and tugged her mouth down to his for a deep kiss. "You'll never regret it. I swear it, love."

"Fate brought me here. I'm not letting you go. You're mine, Gabriel."

"My timely little wallflower," he mused. "You arrived exactly when I needed you most."

Lily laughed, and he kissed her again.

He pushed the ledgers away and lifted her on to the desk. His hands slid beneath the hem of her dress and moved up her thighs. "Let me show you how much I love you," he said against her lips. "Then we'll tell Vi. She was devastated to lose you."

Lily gave into his kiss. She had a man that she loved and new friends. The last few years had been spent trying to find a place that felt like home, only to find her heart two hundred years in the past.

Gabriel unbuttoned his trousers.

Lily stroked him, delighting in the feel of his hard length in her hand.

He rubbed the head through her damp folds, then thrust into her body.

She moaned and clutched his shoulders for balance as he dragged her hips closer to the edge of his desk. "Yes," she said against his lips.

Gabriel pressed his forehead to hers, sharing her breath, then thrust harder. He gripped her hips, holding her in place as he claimed her. "My Lily."

She smiled at his guttural words and pressed a kiss to his lips.

He slipped his hand between their bodies and stroked his fingers over her nub. "Show me your pleasure, love. I want to feel it." He rolled his thumb over her in a firm circle, making her cry out.

Lily shivered as tingles swamped her, tightening her nipples. She pressed kisses to his neck and gave in to the feelings as he drove her higher and higher, until her climax crashed over her, burying her in waves of pleasure.

Distantly, she heard Gabriel cry out against her neck and the muscles of his arms hardened. He shuddered through his own release.

Would it always be like this between them? God, she hoped so.

A sliver of fear for the future threatened to stamp out the glow of happiness she felt. What if his interest eventually waned? *No.* She pushed the thought away. The tenderness she saw as he looked down at her now, their breaths mingling, the love shining in his eyes, told her what her heart already knew. Gabriel was hers. She wouldn't allow anyone to change that.

Gabriel took her mouth in a deep, lingering kiss. "I shall never look at my desk the same way," he said.

Lily laughed. "I think this is an excellent new use for it."

He grinned, and the boyish charm on his face caught her breath. "I can think of several other pieces of furniture in need of this particular treatment."

"Oh, yeah?"

"Indeed. Given time, I'll introduce you to every part of this house and our London townhome."

Our townhome. Lily took his hand when he helped her off the desk. Her heart warmed. For the first time in years, she would have a true home to share with loved ones. That meant almost as much as Gabriel's love.

CHAPTER SIXTEEN

L ATER THAT EVENING, after dinner, they adjourned to the drawing room. Violet and Christian were bent over a game of backgammon, bickering like siblings.

Gabriel had claimed a chair by the fire and pulled Lily down onto his lap. She lay her head on his shoulder and snuggled against him. He'd never felt so content. That Lily chose to stay when she'd had the opportunity to leave and mend the relationship with her family as she had wanted still surprised him. He meant what he said earlier. He would have gone with her. Lily deserved to have everything she wanted in life.

"My family is yours now," he said softly.

"Hmm. In a way, Violet and Christian are like Bellamy and Archer. They certainly bicker like them."

He chuckled. "It would seem that some things will never change, no matter what century one is in. Family...siblings...love."

She fiddled with the knot of his cravat. "Some things are universal."

Indeed. As was another thing. Something that had been on his mind since the moment Lily climbed into his lap and declared her love for him. "Up," he said and helped her to stand. Taking her hand in his, he led her toward the door.

Violet caught his eye, and he gave her a small nod. Her smile was

"Where are we going?" Lily asked as he tugged her into the hall.

He led her up the stairs to the first floor and into the library. Moonlight shone through the windows in long silvery stripes upon the carpet and the fire burned low.

"Gabriel?"

He lit a couple candles and then drew her near the bookshelves. "Here," he said. "This is the place where you first captured my attention, Lily Bennett. Staring up at me in your nightdress with books all around you. I recall that you weren't wearing your spectacles, and your lovely eyes were so bright even in the darkness."

"You remember that?"

He cupped her cheek. "I recall every moment. How soft your skin felt in my hand and smelled like roses. The way you spoke of your siblings and your hopes and dreams. Hopes to one day have a family of your own."

She nodded and pressed a hand over her belly. "One day."

Gabriel feathered his thumb over her cheek, taking a moment to commit every part of this night to memory. The way her caramel curls framed her lovely eyes. The scent of her skin and the pretty gown she wore. The love he felt in his heart for her.

He reached into his pocket and removed the burgundy velvet box that once belonged to his grandmother. He opened it to reveal the gold ring within. Three emeralds circled by diamonds lay side by side, giving the appearance of tiny flowers.

Lily's breath audibly caught. She looked at the ring, then up at him with rounded eyes. "Gabriel?"

"Lily Bennett, would you grant me the honor of becoming my wife?"

Moisture gathered on her lashes as he removed the ring from the box and held it out. She trembled as she lifted her left hand and he slid it onto her ring finger. It was a little loose, but his jeweler could adjust it.

"Are you sure?" she asked.

He chuckled. "I have never been more certain of anything, love."

She stared at the ring for a long moment, then looked up at him.

His stomach swooped. Did she not want this?

The moment he had the thought, Lily launched herself into his arms, peppering his face with kisses. "Yes! Yes, yes, yes!" she cried.

Gabriel wrapped his arms around her and claimed her mouth in a kiss. His heart pounded. Lily was his, and he'd never been happier.

She pulled back and brushed a wayward lock of hair off his forehead. "I love you, Gabriel."

"I love you, too, Lily. For all of time and whatever may come after."

About the Author

Aurrora St. James has been writing romance since she was a teen. Fortunately for the world, those stories will never see the light of day. Now, she loves writing sexy, paranormal romances featuring tough and sometimes dark heroes, women who find their inner strength, and a touch of humor added in for spice. In particular, she enjoys writing both Medieval and Regency romances that whisk readers into the beautiful landscapes of history, where love can overcome anything.

When she's not writing, you'll find her reading, drinking coffee, making her own journals, or watching old B, C, and D-movies. She lives in the Florida jungle with her husband, a slightly crazy dog, and a cat that thinks he's a brontosaurus.

Social Media:
Website: www.aurrorastjames.com
Facebook: facebook.com/AurroraStJamesAuthor
Instagram: instagram.com/aurrorastjames
Pinterest: pinterest.com/ladyaurrora
Bookbub: bookbub.com/authors/aurrora-st-james
Amazon: amazon.com/Aurrora-St.-James/e/B00E46VJD8
Goodreads: goodreads.com/AurroraStJames

Printed in Great Britain
by Amazon

32798848R00109